Now it was her turn

Crystal felt Luke quiver as she traced the intricate shell of his ear with her tongue and tickled the lobe with small nips.

"Stop it, Crystal," he growled.

"Chicken?" she breathed into his exquisitely sensitized ear.

He raised his hand to her lips and traced their fullness. Then he followed her jawline and tangled his fingers in her hair. Even her scalp responded to his caress. Every muscle, bone and fiber of her body prickled with longing.

Oh, how she wanted this man!

THE AUTHOR

Cassie Miles recommends mountain living if you want romance. She and her husband lived in a log cabin in the Colorado Rockies for three years—and every day was filled with wonder and delight.

They now make their home in Denver with their two young daughters. In summer, they follow the girls' little-league baseball team. In winter, they go camping in the snow.

Tongue-Tied

CASSIE MILES

Harlequin Books

TORONTO • NEW YORK • LONDON
AMSTERDAM • PARIS • SYDNEY • HAMBURG
STOCKHOLM • ATHENS • TOKYO • MILAN

Published September 1984

ISBN 0-373-25126-2

Printed in Canada

1

"'SHALL I COMPARE THEE to a summer's day?'" The voice on the cassette tape twanged that immortal question with a broad Texas accent.

"Do I have a choice?" asked Crystal Baxter, speech therapist, with an indulgent grin.

As the speaker cheerfully continued his drawling mutilation of Shakespeare's poetry, Crystal's amusement almost caused her to forget her professional assessment of his speech patterns. The tape finished with: "That's all for this week, Crystal honey. You know, I'm beginning to like this Shakespeare."

"I'll be sure to tell him, Reverend," Crystal replied to the now-silent cassette. She visualized the round red-faced minister who owned that irrepressible Texas twang. *At least,* she thought, *his stutter is well under control.*

She would have recorded her instructions for the following week with comments and compliments, but—as usual—Crystal was doing two things at once: listening to tapes from clients, and hanging wallpaper. At the moment, she was more paperhanger than therapist.

With one hand splayed flat against the wall and the other frantically sponging, Crystal struggled with an unwieldy length of self-adhesive paper. The ten-foot-high ceilings in her comfortable Victorian home had not been plumb since Denver's gold rush, which made this modest redecoration an exacting and difficult task. She had only planned to cover two walls of the large parlor that served as her office, and one of those walls was mostly windows. Yet, after two hours of back-breaking labor, the primed expanse that still loomed before her, denuded of pictures, seemed as blank and vast as the poop deck of the *Queen Mary* in dry dock.

She dangled precariously from an aluminum ladder, trying to match the delicate primrose-and-gray paisley. Swirls of pattern blurred before her tawny eyes. Each time she forced the paper to fit, another section came unglued. Frustrated, Crystal wished for two extra arms like the Hindu god, Shiva.

This was not an unusual thought for the twenty-six-year-old auburn-haired speech therapist. With doctoral studies in Speech Pathology, her own burgeoning therapy practice, upkeep of the old family manor and volunteer work at the Children's Museum, Crystal often juggled more responsibilities than most people could manage.

She firmly affixed the upper corners of the wallpaper and stepped down the ladder. The left side buckled. She attacked, gamely hammering out the air bubbles with the heel of her small hand. The lower edge of the paper slapped against the oaken woodwork, leaving a sticky residue while miraculously refusing to stick.

"Self-adhesive, my eye," she muttered. "*No* adhesive is more like it."

Throwing her slim body full against the wallpaper, Crystal pressed the bulky sheet down in wide overhead arcs. The cotton material of her oversized, blue work shirt clung to the surface of the wallpaper. She pinned a reluctant edge with her denim-clad knee. It was an all-out battle between woman and wall-paper—and wallpaper was winning.

As if timed for inconvenience, the doorbell buzzed. "Not now," she moaned, hoping that whoever it was would go away. Her appointment calendar was completely clear, and she was looking forward to an interruption-free afternoon.

The bell screamed again, more prolonged and insistent. Crystal narrowed her eyes and pictured the entrance to her slate-blue house with the neat white trim. What if it was a client?

She imagined wispy Mrs. Patton standing on the wide veranda and jabbing at the bell. Can a buzzer sound desperate? That high-strung lady's agoraphobia was complicated by a babyish lisp, the impediment Crystal was treating. What if Mrs. Patton had finally braved the supermarket and needed Crystal's warm, supportive praises? It might even be Marilyn James with four-year-old Michael in tow, coming to report her son's first coherent utterances. Or it could be any one of her stutterers having a relapse.

The buzzer whined. What was it Crystal's father always said? Doctors and plumbers never have a moment's privacy. She added speech therapists to that list, conceded defeat in the war of the wallpaper and went to answer the door.

Through the leaded glass oval in the carved mahogany door, she spied on her intruder—a tall broad-shouldered man. A familiarity in the set of his jaw and the arch of his eyebrow kept her standing in the shadow and staring. Who was he? Definitely not a client. The impeccable fit of his tan linen suit emphasized that he was neither repairman nor newspaper carrier. Perhaps he was another therapist, someone she'd met at a convention. Crystal dismissed that possibility as soon as it surfaced. She would never have forgotten such an undeniably handsome colleague.

Even in the dry August heat, he appeared cool and poised. Yet, his hands betrayed a restlessness. They raked through his thick, sun-streaked blond hair that fell back exactly into place in casual layers. He fidgeted impatiently, loosened his regimental striped necktie of blue and brown and stabbed once again at her doorbell.

Standing just beyond his peripheral vision, Crystal jumped inadvertently at the loud sounding of the buzzer and reached for the brass doorknob. "May I help you?"

His eyes were blue, a deep and dreamy azure, and his gaze slid over her sloppy shirt and baggy Levi's before coming to rest on her high-cheekboned, lightly freckled, smudged face. His resonant baritone held a hint of amusement. "I am looking for C. J. Baxter."

"You've found her. I am Crystal Jane Baxter."

She self-consciously ran paste-filled fingers through her unruly, russet hair and adjusted her tumbled-down ponytail. Her youthful appearance created a credibility gap, and she was aware that in her wallpapering outfit she probably looked no more than seventeen. Still, the deepening of lightly etched laugh lines around his startling blue eyes irritated her.

He pointed to the brass plaque mounted above the doorbell. "C. J. Baxter, Speech Language Pathologist. May I come in?" He finished untying the Windsor knot and allowed his necktie to hang loosely down the pale-blue shirtfront. "Or do you prefer to conduct speech therapy on the front porch?"

His speaking pattern held a barely noticeable hesitation that Crystal had come to recognize as indicative of a minor speech problem. If he was coming to her as a legitimate client, this introduction was indeed unfortunate. He had caught her without her professional armor, and his teasing manner already indicated a lack of respect.

She tried to infuse her voice with intelligent self-assurance. "An immediate appointment is out of the question." She thought of her wallpaper. "And I really have to get back to what I was doing. Or else I'm going to come all unglued."

"Unglued?"

"Literally," she asserted as she inwardly winced at her poor choice of words.

"I tried all afternoon to reach you," he said. "But your answering service wouldn't put me through."

"That was my instruction. I was only to be disturbed in case of emergency."

"I think this qualifies."

An emergency? She judged otherwise. She had seen too many real emergencies—people with terror paralyzing their throats as they strangled on their own words. What did he know of emergencies? He was like a well-heeled hypochondriac tugging at the aqua gown of a brain surgeon.

She had to smile at the presumptuousness of her comparison. Paperhanging hardly qualified as a life-or-death operation. "Would you briefly explain the nature of your emergency?"

"Here? On the porch?" He peered up and down her tree-lined street.

She followed his gaze to a bronze Ferrari that glistened in the hot sun. His car? "You might be more comfortable here," she suggested dryly. "At least you could protect your hubcaps."

"It's just that I had expected a bit more confidentiality. In any case, I insist that you see me now. I won't ask twice."

His electric-blue eyes drilled right through her, so accusing and challenging that she almost slammed the door in his face. Then, he displayed a paradoxical sensitivity in a one-word appeal. "Please."

She had no choice but to relent. Her ethics would never allow her to refuse a cry for help. "Do you mind waiting?"

"Not if I can use your telephone to contact my office."

She thought of the long, blank wall and the morass of wallpaper. "It could take quite a long time," she warned as she opened the door to admit him. "But you are welcome to read my back issues of *National Geographic*."

As he entered the house and glanced from old-time photographs of Baxter forefathers to a modernistic brass coat rack to a bright floral display in a carnival glass vase, he sighed with relief. "Doesn't look at all like a clinic."

"It's my family home. I live here as well as work here," she told him defensively. "If you're looking for high technology, you had better take your emergency elsewhere."

"I think I've found what I'm looking for."

She led him down a short corridor into the anteroom, which served as her reception area, and stood behind the delicate Chippendale desk. Her pen hovered over a leather-bound appointment book. "Your name?"

"Luke Todhunter. I'm sure we've met socially."

"Or at least we've attended the same soirees," she said primly, recognizing his surname as one of the old, wealthy families of Denver. Like her own. Despite the booming growth of her hometown, the cadre of natives formed a small, sometimes exclusive group. That probably accounted for her vague recognition when she first saw him.

With a flourish, she wrote his name on the blank appointment page. "I had a Karen Todhunter in one of my classes at the university."

"My cousin. She recommended you. Said you were a tough teacher."

"Teacher's assistant," she corrected as she presented him with a registration card. "Please fill in all the blanks, Mr. Todhunter."

"Call me Luke. We native Coloradoans should be on a first name basis."

"Certainly, Luke. We have so much in common with the rustlers and potato farmers from whom we descended."

Gallantly disregarding the sticky paste, he shook her hand. Crystal was pleasantly surprised by his strong, leathery grip. He looked too slick and citified to have the hands of an outdoorsman.

"Which were you?" he asked. "A farmer or a cowboy?"

"Neither. Great-great-grandfather was a merchant. We're city folk, except for my father. Denver is too calm for him. He and mother are pioneering new frontiers in Alaska. He's a geologist."

"Sam Baxter," Luke said quickly. "I met him briefly

at an environmentalist conference a few years back. And I remember something unusual about you Baxters. Aren't you all named for minerals and precious stones?"

"Garnet, Jade and my brother, Flint." Her withering glare told him that she'd heard every possible joke about rockheads, rolling stones and chips off the old block.

Still, he commented. "I don't know about your sisters and brothers, but I think you were misnamed. Crystal is hard and cold. Unfeeling. With the reddish cast to your hair and the fire in your eyes, your name should be more translucent." His dispassionate enumeration of her characteristics left her unsure as to whether he was teasing or complimenting. "You're like a ruby or a fine claret. Scarlet?"

"Thanks, Rhett." A crimson flush started at her throat and spread to her cheeks. "If you will excuse me, I'll try to complete my other business quickly. You may use the phone on the desk."

She slipped through the door to her office, closed it firmly and turned to the messy business at hand. Wallpaper.

The piece she had struggled with earlier was almost completely peeled from the wall, drooping like a lop-eared rabbit. She draped the dry length about her shoulders to keep it from bunching in an unmanageable heap on the cluttered floor. Then she pulled and peeled and coaxed at the gooey lower edge. She'd just detached the entire strip when she heard a knock at the door.

"Don't come in," she shouted. Her credibility would be shot if he discovered her in this weird parody of a snake charmer.

"Crystal? Can you give me some idea of how long I need to wait?"

She stumbled toward the door, dragging a train of paisley. The aluminum ladder intervened and she yanked too vigorously. Her feet tangled, and she sat down hard on the dropcloth. Her loud gasp and muttered oath prompted him to open the door.

"Are you all right?" he asked.

She disengaged one hand to massage her lower spine. "Let's just say that I hurt more than my pride."

She waited for him to sneer or laugh, but instead found a sincere concern as he helped her rise. "You've done very well so far. It really takes four hands to hang wallpaper."

"Oh, the wonders I could accomplish with four hands and another twelve hours in every day," she said with exasperation.

"Might be easier to share the work. I know a dozen men who would gladly volunteer."

"Silently? And without time-consuming obligations?"

"Nothing's free, Crystal. Think how hard it would be to find clothes for those extra two arms." He removed his jacket and rolled up his sleeves. "It's in my best interest to see that you're done with this before midnight."

She thought of her own best interests and decided that he had already seen her at her worst. Though it was unorthodox to recruit new clients to hang wallpaper, Luke Todhunter had already transgressed normal procedures.

He wetted the sponge in a plastic bucket of water and assumed a place on the ladder. With efficient strokes, he worked a new piece into place. "I'll hold the top and you start from the bottom. Does the pattern match?''

With amazement, she replied that it did. "But it's lumpy on this side."

He instructed her to smooth over the air bubbles. "Delicately," he cautioned. "Think of a caress, not an assault."

The surprising ease of her task convinced her that his suggestive comparison was valid. Her earlier problem had been in fighting the paisley—the rape of the wallpaper.

"Why didn't you hire a paperhanger?" he asked.

"The earliest they could fit me in was two weeks from yesterday. Besides, I am a totally self-sufficient person." Though her statement of confidence rang true, her hands were all thumbs. She had the easier job of measuring and cutting, but she bungled clumsily. Her edges were ragged, and she was covered with slimy paste.

In contrast, there was a soothing competence to Luke's movements, a graceful economy. For a big man, he displayed an uncommon deftness. As he stretched and reached, the cloth of his shirt outlined the broad musculature of his back.

She observed him with an attention that slipped beyond the casual as she admired the bulge of his long biceps and the taut swell of his haunches. Her ringside view confirmed the most flattering of her first impressions. Even from the back, Luke was an extremely handsome man.

Under his skillful hands, the white wall bloomed with pattern. Crystal rationalized that his height made the work look simple. She figured an advantage of at least seven inches over her own five-and-a-half-foot stature. That, plus his obvious experience. How old was he? Mid-thirties, she guessed. Her eyes strayed to his ringless fingers. Was he married? That was none of her business, she reminded herself, unless his age and marital status related to his therapy. She aimed for detachment with a banal, nonthreatening question. "What do you do for a living?"

"Hanging paper isn't far out of my line, but the kind of paper I work with is covered with legalese. I'm an attorney specializing in contract law and water rights."

A flash of recall finally identified him for her. She had seen him in the local newspaper. He was well-known for his protest against Coyote Creek Dam, a position that Crystal deemed foolishly idealistic. Though she agreed that the proposed dam would wreak unfortunate devastation on hundreds of acres of national forest, she reacted as a realistic city woman. Increased water supply for Denver was an unavoidable necessity.

Grudgingly, she admired Luke's tenacity in spearheading the opposition. His legal research had unearthed a plethora of obscure settlers' rights and treaties with the Arapahoe Indians. Petitions and mandates and bumper stickers poured from his office, effectively garnering support from environmentalists. His reward might be a political plum.

"So, Mr. Todhunter," she said. "Are you going to run for Congress? Is the new representative from Jefferson County papering my wall?"

"That may be entirely up to you." He patted the last corner of paisley print into place and surveyed his work with satisfaction. "That was good therapy. I don't get to use my hands as much as I'd like. I congratulate you, doctor. The patient is at ease."

"I'm not a doctor. Not until I complete my dissertation." She stepped back to the center of the room to see the full effect of her new decor. "You don't think it's too bright? Too busy?"

He joined her. "It's perfect. Tasteful and Victorian, like the rest of your home."

Standing beside him, she was uncomfortably aware of his height advantage. The top of her head barely grazed his chin level. As she stood on tiptoe to compensate, she pivoted off balance and accidentally brushed his upper arm, leaving a smear of glue.

"I'm so sorry." She daubed at his shirt sleeve with sticky fingers. "I don't know why I'm so klutzy today. Just look at the two of us. You did most of the work, but you're fresh as a daisy. How did I get to be such a mess?"

"It's your room," he said, watching as she worsened the smudge. "I only worked on it. You got involved."

She grabbed the sponge to repair his shirt and instead created a gigantic, wet glop. "Oh no, I'm demolishing your shirt. It's a good thing we're done."

"Correction. We haven't yet started. As much as I enjoyed the physical labor, I didn't come here as a handyman."

"Right." She glared at the mess she'd made of his arm, which he now held away from his body at a dripping right angle. "You'd better take off that shirt and let me wash it. I don't want to be responsible for a stain."

"It's all right, Crystal. I don't mind."

"You can't possibly be comfortable with that gunk slopping all over your arm. Now, take it off. I'll find something else for you to wear." Her tone was firm and commanding, the same voice she used when dealing with uncooperative children. "I insist."

"Well, yes ma'am. I guess I'd better get used to taking orders from my therapist." His fingers undid the buttons quickly. Too quickly. Crystal was unprepared for his virile expanse of well-muscled chest covered with a thick, curling pelt of soft, dark brown hair. His tanned flesh beckoned her to touch, to run her hands down his sinewed arms and feel the warm hardness.

Luke's appealing masculinity defied her father's saying that naked men look like plucked chickens. Naked? How long had it been since a half-naked man stood in her office? Never. Never in her inner sanctum. Her breath quickened.

"Amber," he said. "Not Crystal. Not Scarlet. You're like amber, golden and glowing."

She snatched the shirt from his hands and mumbled, "I'll throw this in the washer and be right back."

She hurried to the laundry room just beyond the kitchen and leaned against the Maytag trying to regain her composure. The mental photograph of his lean torso would not disappear. She massaged her temple, trying to erase the indelible picture. It was ironic, she thought. He had come to her for help, but she was the one with a behavior problem. She remembered his comment about the wallpaper: he only worked on it. She got involved.

That had to be the answer, she thought as her mental processes groped for normalcy. He was the type who would always escape unscathed, the breed of man who drove a Ferrari. He was a charismatic politician whose appearance of suave sincerity came as second nature to him. She was the extreme opposite, always battling to control her enthusiasm and maintain a respectable aura of detachment. As she hurtled headlong into life, constantly overwhelmed and sympathetic, Crystal couldn't help getting her hands dirty.

She fiddled with the dials on the washer and held the shirt before her. It seemed huge in comparison to her dainty garments. Many years had passed since she helped her mother launder the clothing of her father and brother. Impulsively, she crumpled the blue material and held it close to her face, inhaling the mysterious, spiced aroma of his masculinity.

The intimate sensation of caring for a man rose painfully in her breast. She spoke to his shirt. "I'm much too busy to be interested. After I've got my doctorate, I'll put my personal life into order. And don't think you'll get around me with sweet speeches about glowing amber."

She flung the shirt into the washer and slammed the lid. The rhythmic syncopation of the machine echoed an imagined response: too late, too late. Don't wait, too late.

She ignored its churning and raced up the back stairwell to her parents' vacant bedroom. Her father was as tall as Luke, but not nearly as broad. She found a stretchy knit to accommodate the difference in shoulder size and returned to her office.

In her absence, he'd rearranged all the furniture. It was almost exactly the placement she preferred, and she remembered the strenuous job of clearing the area near the wall. There were advantages, she thought, to having a man around the house.

She thanked him, her eyes slipping swiftly from his gaze, and held out her father's shirt. Even that brief glimpse of his bared chest caused a giddy effervescence to bubble in her brain. "If you will excuse me, Luke, I'd better clean myself up before we discuss your treatment."

"Perhaps we could talk over dinner," he suggested while he slipped the shirt over his head. The knit material stretched across his broad chest like a second skin.

"Sorry, I have plans for this evening," she truthfully replied. Though her agenda only included an appointment with her textbooks and revisions of her doctoral dissertation, she presented it as a firm commitment. "I probably won't have time for dinner at all."

He eyed her slender curves beneath the ill-fitting shirt and Levi's. "Doesn't look to me like you could afford to miss many meals."

"Probably not," she agreed. "But I keep myself running with constant doses of black coffee. There's a pot in the kitchen, down the hall to your left. Please help yourself while I change."

Though he hadn't moved a muscle, she stepped back a pace. He seemed to be getting too close. His blue-eyed gaze made inroads in her carefully schooled equanimity. With as much poise as she could muster, Crystal fled her newly paislied office.

2

UP THE STAIRS and into her bedroom she sprinted, chased by the devilish twinkle of bright blue eyes and the suggestive, masculine echo of his baritone. Why was her mouth so dry? Why this adolescent blushing?

When she had admitted him to her office, she hadn't intended to open the door to her personal life. What Pandora's box was this?

Fading sunlight lit the bower of leaves outside her window. She glanced at her digital bedroom clock: 5:09. There were at least two more hours until darkness, and Crystal instinctively knew she must bid farewell to Luke before then. Or else, what? Would she turn into a pumpkin?

She shucked off her work clothes and dove into the shower in the adjoining bathroom. Pulsating jets of water refreshed her. Warm rivulets flowed between her breasts and into the delicate indentation of her navel. She offered her face to the spray, cleansing every trace of sticky, unconfirmed longing.

"Amber," she reflected with melancholy regret. "I'm sure he was only being polite, and I'd be a dope to take him seriously. Anyway, he's a client, or almost a client. It would be professional death to be involved with someone I'm supposed to be treating."

She briskly toweled the angular curves of her slim

body and chastised herself for her unexpected reaction to Luke. "I'm turning into a horny old maid. I let a few kind words and a gorgeous set of pectorals drive me right up the wallpaper."

She vowed to make short work of Luke's "emergency"—whatever it was—and return unscathed to the safe cocoon of her daily schedule.

It took all her energy to keep up her regular pace, and she was too close to her goals now to be tempted to stray. Though friends advised her to stop and smell the flowers, Crystal complained of hay fever. She viewed luncheons and parties and vacations as interruptions.

"When I've got my Ph.D., I'll take some time off," she told herself firmly. "I could visit my parents in Alaska."

An unbidden thought popped into her consciousness. *Or maybe that would be the time to give Mr. Todhunter a call. Take him out to dinner? Tell him I have free tickets to a play?*

She sighed wistfully and buried thoughts that she deemed self-indulgent. She owed everything—her self-image, her livelihood, her very existence—to speech therapy. Nothing must interfere with her goals.

A quick blow-dry tamed the heavy, auburn mane, which she pinned into a twist. She dabbed rouge on lips she'd always thought were too thin. A fingerful of taupe eye shadow highlighted her wide-set, golden-brown eyes, and a brush of blush played down the rather severe cheekbones.

As if to counteract her first impression on him, she selected a tailored, businesslike outfit—kelly-green linen with white piping at the neck and wrist. She fastened the thin white belt one notch tighter than the last time she'd worn the dress. Those extra hours she wished for always seemed to be stolen from the dinner table.

With shoulders squared, Crystal headed downstairs. Her step was light and confident, and her correct posture projected an image of intelligent alertness. Her stomach growled.

The scene that greeted her in the kitchen was pleasantly domestic. Luke sat at the butcher block table reading a magazine from her waiting room. His hand cradled a steaming mug of coffee. Crystal's tomcat, a black-and-white spotted shorthair, twined round his trouser leg. "Are you sure we can't go out?" Luke asked. "I'm starving from all that manual labor."

Crystal poured herself a cup of coffee from the pot on the buttery yellow counter. "I've heard that hunger sharpens the senses. Perhaps, we can make better progress with your therapy on empty stomachs."

"I've heard that lack of food acts as an aphrodisiac."

"In that case, I'll allow time for a snack. Homemade zucchini cake? It's a gift from one of my clients with an overproductive garden."

She cut and served the cake briskly, glad for the opportunity to assuage her appetite. The same crispness characterized her next statement. "Now, Luke, tell me about your emergency."

"I hope you don't make love the same way you conduct your interviews." He took a sip of coffee and smiled across the rim of the mug. "There's a certain lack of foreplay in that first question."

She choked on her cake. "Let's get one thing straight before we go any further. If I am to be your therapist, we will have no more talk of dinner dates, aphrodisiacs and foreplay. Is that clearly understood?"

"Could we at least drool over the pictures in *National Geographic* together?" He held up the magazine he had been reading.

"Please don't be difficult." Knowing that a first therapy session caused great tension for the client, Crystal was willing to make some allowances for Luke's behavior. It was important to engage in relaxing small talk and to gain his trust, but it was equally vital to set working limits. These applied to her own actions as well, she thought ruefully. She had already transgressed normal propriety by accepting his help with the wallpaper and sitting here in the kitchen as if they were a couple of old friends. And, of course, there was the problem of his shirt.

"Try to understand," she said. "Though my introduction to you was not exactly the epitome of professionalism, I am not generally in the habit of stripping the clothing off my new clients."

His raised eyebrows indicated amusement. "I can sympathize. I once had an attractive female client walk into my office just as I was changing into my tennis shorts."

"You're doing it again," she warned.

"Sorry. I just wanted you to know that you're not the only one to be caught with your pants down." He raised his hand to silence her objection. "That was the last time. I promise. I just couldn't leave off the punch line."

"As long as we can maintain a more sedate attitude in the future, there is nothing to apologize for."

As he leaned across the table, the material of the knit shirt stretched to the maximum and revealed the

bulge of his firm biceps. "Actually, I'm glad that
everything happened the way it did. I've been hesitat-
ing for years about seeking therapy. This casual, unorthodox approach makes me feel that I haven't made
a mistake in coming to you."

"Nonetheless, there are limitations." Though his
sincere compliment pleased her immeasureably, she
consciously kept her distance. Clinically, she again
noted the very unobtrusive hesitation in his speech.
"I have a feeling that you know what I mean by limits."

"Henceforth, I will be a Boy Scout. Clean in thought,
word and deed." He raised his left hand in a three-
fingered salute. "Let me amend that to word and deed
only. My thoughts are my own business."

"Were you ever in scouting?" She was grateful to
find a neutral topic to begin drawing him into conversation.

"Not for long. I got bored. When you grow up on a
ranch, cookouts don't hold much fascination."

"Tell me about the ranch. I was a city kid, even
when Denver couldn't be called much more than an
overgrown village."

As she listened, she acknowledged the validity of
his no-foreplay complaint. It was unfeeling of her to
leap so threateningly to the heart of his problem. She
was usually so careful with the people who came to
her for help, solicitous and considerate of their fragile
egos. Possibly, her afternoon with Luke had caused
her to regard him more as a friend than a client. With
a mental slap on the wrist, her thinking readjusted,
and her talk drifted along casual, conventional lines.
The hot summer weather. The new USFL professional
football team. Skiing.

The verbal procedure she used was not unlike a skilled seduction, though she had never before considered the process in that light. A gentle teasing and cajoling relaxed the client until they could together confront the problem. Her questions drew him out, and she learned that Luke was not only a competent paperhanger, but also an able cook, gardener and tailor. He had learned a full complement of domestic skills at the knee of a liberated mother who believed little boys should be able to fend for themselves.

Crystal cut off a tiny piece of cake for her cat. "Here you go, Rory. I named him Rorschach because his markings remind me of the ink blot test."

Luke squinted at the black-and-white cat whose yellow eyes reflected pure pleasure at the unusual treat. "That big spot near his neck looks like a hawk in flight about to pounce on that little squiggle of a chipmunk. What does that tell you about me?"

"You are obviously paranoid. The victim of delusions, confusions and contusions. Maybe you were potty trained too early."

"I take it you're not a Freudian."

"Not a Freudian. Not a shrink. That's not my training. My therapies are concerned more with behavioral results."

"No analysis required?" he asked with mock disappointment. "Too bad. I was looking forward to telling you all my fantasies."

She smoothly sidestepped his possible innuendo. "Though it's sometimes instructive to seek out the root of the speech problem, that's not really my job." She sipped her coffee. "Suppose you broke your leg. I wouldn't take the X rays or set the bone. My work would be to see that the limb worked properly again."

"Mind if I get myself a glass of milk?"

She pushed back her chair, but he waved her back into her seat. "I'll find it."

He served himself—a simple act that tugged at Crystal's heartstrings with the familiarity it implied. He didn't need to ask the location of the glasses, but knew intuitively that they were kept in the cupboard to the right of the sink.

He returned to the table. "Your comparison interests me. What if the orthopedic surgeon goofed? What if the broken bone healed incorrectly?"

"If the patient failed to respond to my treatment, I would refer him to another specialist who dealt with the specific problem. Maybe a psychiatrist. Maybe an otologist."

"Otologist?"

"Ear doctor," she explained.

"Right." He leaned back in his chair. "I haven't had much experience with doctors."

"I didn't think you had." She surveyed his physique. As close as she could tell, he was in perfect condition. "Let me enlighten you. I am a Speech Language Pathologist. I have my Clinical Certificate of Competence, which means I've completed course work equivalent to an M.A. plus in-field training plus a national exam. And I am working on my Ph.D. in Speech Pathology."

Since many of the people Crystal worked with were professionals like Luke, she was often required to trot out her credentials. The listing was less impressive than she liked, and she yearned for those three small letters, P-H-D, after her name. She ended the recitation with a statistic she thought he might find pertinent. "I have an eighty-four percent success rate with fluency disorders."

"Can you cure fluency disorders?"

"Not in the sense that it completely disappears. When I refer to success, I mean a significant improvement in controlling and accepting the physical impediment."

A reflex twitch at the corner of his mouth betrayed his discomfort, but all he said was, "I'm impressed. My cousin Karen mentioned your positive results with people who have that particular speech problem."

"Stuttering?" she probed, feeling like the hawk he'd seen in Rorschach's markings about to pounce.

"Yes. That's it." He took his last gulp of milk and concentrated on swallowing. He wouldn't even say that word.

Crystal recognized embarrassment in the tense workings of Luke's jaw and the detached haze that settled over his features. He wasn't the sort of man who would take his handicap lightly, and she realized for the first time how difficult it must have been for him to ask for her help.

She lightly touched his arm and said in a reassuring voice, "I can help you, Luke. Please trust me."

She sensed his inner turmoil, a desperation she knew intimately, and declared an end to foreplay. "How long have you been a stutterer?" she asked softly.

TRUST. That small word encompassed a huge concept.

The struggle raging within Luke Todhunter robbed him of quick response. *How long have I been a stutterer? Forever,* he thought, *condemned to a life sentence in an eternal inferno that even Dante could not imagine.* Luke's subconscious mind was a bleak, desolate battlefield strewn with parched bones. Dead words and lost relationships. He experienced the fearful tightening in his throat and knew that normal speech was impossible.

Whom could he trust? This wide-eyed, intelligent woman whose expertise made her sympathetic to his problem? Would she pity him? He despised the compassion of others. Too often he had allowed himself to be vulnerable in the presence of a woman and discovered her motherly pity when at last his stutter revealed itself. Her eyes would soften, and her passionate embrace would turn to a comforting pat. Such a cruel kindness. He hated women's tenderhearted concern and kept himself distant from those whose high opinion he valued.

He almost preferred the vicious laughter from the children he grew up with. "L-l-luke," they cried in remembered chorus. "What's the c-c-capital of C-c-colorado? D-d-denver."

How many fistfights had there been on the playground? How many times had he brushed away friendship, fearing it would end in a stammer?

The stutter had forced him into early independence. Luke had chosen solitary pursuits, spent hours developing his body and reading until loneliness drove him to a solution. By avoiding the words that triggered his handicap, Luke could disguise his stutter. He could engage in brief conversations strictly by willpower, carefully choosing his words. No one ever guessed the supreme effort that went into each simple exchange. As his confidence grew, he cautiously inserted the problem sounds until his speech was nearly normal. The only situation he had been unable to conquer was public speaking. Every time he appeared before a group, the stutter reappeared. And this was the emergency that had brought him to Crystal Baxter's quaint, Victorian door.

The kickoff to his political campaign was scheduled for a week from Friday, ten days hence, at a town meeting. The prospect was harrowing. In nightmares Luke saw a sea of complacent faces, heard a smattering of applause that turned to laughter when his resonant voice declaimed like Porky Pig, "Th-th-that's all, f-f-folks."

"Luke?" She called him back from his private hell, her voice echoing across the chasm of silence. "Let's talk in my office."

"How did you know I had that particular speech problem?"

"Stuttering?" she said mercilessly. "Elementary, my dear Todhunter. You have a characteristic hesitation. Plus almost everything I've read about you in the news has been quoted from written, not oral, sources. By the way, I don't agree with your stand on Coyote Creek Dam."

"Why not? The dam will destroy thousands of years' worth of indigenous growth. What right have we to flood those hundreds of acres? To wipe out the natural environment of this state?"

"Denver needs water," she said simply. "If your argument were drawn to the logical conclusion, we humans would forego the right to chop down trees for houses and fuel. We should never have proliferated across the plains to begin with. You're a Colorado native. I would think you'd be more sympathetic to the pioneering point of view."

"It's not the same. The first settlers used their ex-

pertise to the maximum. We should do no less with
our advanced technology." His eloquence on the subject returned his self-confident poise. He recognized
the reprieve she'd granted with her change of topic
and appreciated her sensitivity. Perhaps she was the
person he could finally trust.

How different she was from his expectations! From
his cousin's description, he'd thought he'd find a ma-
tronly professor in sensible shoes. Instead, he was
greeted by this spunky, auburn-haired gamine. Even
in that crazy, oversized work shirt she had been an
attractive, desirable woman. If the situation had been
less critical, he would have bypassed her reputed skill
as a therapist and pursued her as a woman. "Have
you seen the dam site?" he asked.

"I suppose I have. It's southeast of Granger's Bluff
on the Platte, isn't it?"

"But have you actually walked that land?" His blue
eyes reflected the glory of a clear, Colorado sky.
"Have you seen the beaver lodges or heard the whir
of hummingbird wings? Have you smelled the scent
of pine after a spring rainfall?"

"'Shall I compare thee to a summer's day?'" she
repeated the speech exercise of her plump minister.
"You're quite poetic, Luke."

"I hoped to be convincing, to touch your city
woman's soul with the magnificence of Colorado. Let
me take you there, Crystal. Let me show you the
mountains as I see them."

"I am a native," she reminded him. "I know my
way around the Rockies."

"When was the last time you hiked without purpose in those hills?"

Her expression showed him that like so many

others who grew up in Denver she took the magnificent locale for granted. "I think I'm offering a fair trade," he continued. "You fix my speech problem. I'll show you what you've been missing."

"If you're this persistent with every member of the loyal opposition, it could be a long campaign."

"I'm not asking for a vote," he said. "I'm asking for a date."

"That would be a most irregular form of therapy," she chided. "Shall we continue our discussion in my office?"

He followed, dreading the confrontation that her office implied. Maybe he didn't really need therapy, he thought as he admired her slim shapely legs. The nagging fear of failure reasserted itself in his conscious mind. It was important that he not appear foolish in her eyes. Yet, he knew that inevitably he would stammer. The monster would appear as always to destroy a budding relationship.

"Tell me, Luke," she said, reading his mind. "Why is it that the challenging, young politician does not come equipped with a docile wife and 2.5 children? Or are you married?"

"Never found the right woman," he lied. There had been any number of suitable conjugal candidates, but he had always held them at arm's length. He wouldn't allow anyone to penetrate his defenses and see him as he really was. A wave of nervousness washed through him. He was about to expose that inner self to Crystal. Could he trust her?

She avoided the desk and indicated a comfortable, conversational area of the office. As she sat and crossed her supple legs, she glanced at her wristwatch.

"Just like a therapist," he said. "Is this the beginning of my fifty-minute hour? I suppose these wingback chairs are supposed to put the patient at ease."

"Stop being so self-involved, Luke," she gently teased. "Two and a half million people in the United States are stutterers. We're sitting here because I'm more comfortable. And stop thinking of yourself as a patient. I'm not a miracle worker. All I do is give you the tools. You have to do the work."

"All right." He settled back on the burgundy velvet wingback, just about as relaxed as a condemned man going to the electric chair. "Let's get on with it."

"My father used to say that you could give a man a hammer, but until he trusted his thumb to hold the nail, he couldn't build a house. We'll start at the beginning. When was the first time you remember stuttering?"

"Show-and-tell in kindergarten." Even now the memory made him wince. "I had brought a model train engine, and I couldn't say the letter *t*. There might have been a problem before that, but I wasn't aware of it."

"Were you referred to a therapist?"

"We're talking about ancient history, Crystal. Speech therapists and social workers were not a regular part of the curriculum. My parents sent me to a Mrs. Coggins who was an elocutionist."

"And what happened?"

"She was a sweet, gray-haired lady and she meant well."

He vividly recalled the long sessions in Mrs. Coggins's eccentric parlor that always smelled of violets. A metronome on the piano ticked off the seconds as she urged him to speak from the diaphragm, illustrating by patting that mysterious place beneath her ample bosom. She told him to round his tones and—for pity's sake, Luke—slow down.

He had droned out rolling vowels. And learned to clip his consonants. He had memorized Hamlet's Speech to the Players. In Mrs. Coggins's educated accents, Luke had orated elegantly, finally learning to match stilted rhetorical gestures to his speech. She finally pronounced him cured and arranged for a family recitation to display her pupil's talents.

He would never forget the shocked expression on her face when he rose to address his audience and stammered uncontrollably.

"Let's just say that Mrs. Coggins didn't work out," he summarized the dismal experience. "I've never had another therapist."

"May I compliment you. Your control is superior." She cut to the heart of the matter. "What exactly is the emergency you spoke of?"

"My political campaign. A week from this Friday I have to address a town meeting in Golden. The only time my problem is sure to reappear is when I speak in public."

"You're giving me ten whole days?" she asked incredulously. With that type of deadline, it was difficult to believe he was sincerely interested in treatment. More likely, he was setting himself up to fail.

Her lips thinned to a determined line. She would help him in spite of himself. "I guess we have no more time to spend on reminiscence. You've already told me what I need to know. Since your stutter is usually controlled, we can eliminate physical causes."

"Isn't that wonderful," he said with heavy sarcasm. "It's all in my head. Is that what you're saying?"

"Not exactly. The explanation is not that simple."

"Do you realize what this could do to me politically? Who will vote for a crazy man who can't say his own name in front of more than three people. Maybe I'd better keep my hat on my head and not in the ring."

"What? And let people like me pass the legislation for Coyote Creek Dam?" She refused to let him off the hook. "The town meeting will be an excellent test of the effectiveness of our therapy."

"What if it doesn't work? What if I get up there behind the bunting-draped podium and can't talk?"

"You'll simply have to trust me."

She allowed him a moment to absorb her statement, aware that an important decision was being made behind those liquid blue eyes. She didn't expect a lifetime of barriers to crumble in an instant, but he had to agree to try. The dam he aggressively opposed was a good metaphor for his situation. She guessed that a reservoir of emotions—fear and love and anger and joy—were dammed within him by his stutter, and she had to dismantle that wall brick by brick. He was too good a person to be captive to his impediment.

"Okay," he said carefully. "I'm in your hands."

"I'm going to insist on a time commitment. Shall we say four hours a day for the next ten days? I can clear my calendar in the morning from eight until ten and in the evening after five."

"Is it really necessary? I have some important work coming up next week."

"That's just the beginning of my demands," she said brusquely. Her time was as valuable as his. She was robbing herself of the hours she usually set aside for editing her doctoral dissertation and, as usual, her dinner hours. "How many minutes in your life have you spent stuttering? I don't think your therapy time will be near equal."

"All right." He raised his hands in resignation. "We'll start tomorrow morning."

"Wrong again, Todhunter. We're starting tonight. In the next hour, I will teach you the basic techniques." She jumped out of her chair and hurried to the reception room to fetch her appointment book. She returned, sat and scribbled his name in the empty spaces. "We're also going to have to find some public-speaking opportunities."

"Why? The town meeting should be sufficiently embarrassing."

"I never want to hear that again." Her gaze was steady and determined. "The town meeting will be a terrific success. And you need all the practice you can get before then."

She returned to her appointment book. "This coming Monday I have an evening meeting of DSD, Dysfluent Speakers of Denver. It's a small group. All stutterers. You will speak to them."

"In just five days?"

"It will make an excellent test case. And I'll have a chance to videotape your performance."

"Videotape?" he yelped. "What for?"

"Don't act like you've never been on camera. I saw you on the evening news."

"That was in my office. With one reporter and a cameraman. Not talking to a bunch of weirdos with speech problems."

"My, my, our prejudices are showing. Do you think that all stutterers are somehow odd or crazy? May I remind you that Winston Churchill, one of the great orators of our time, was a stutterer. Demosthenes, King George the Fourth, and Moses were stutterers. Believe me, you are in illustrious company. Besides, if you are going to be a candidate, you'd better get used to videotape."

He settled back in his chair, muscular arms folded across his chest. His posture said: show me.

Not an auspicious start, she thought, but she had not expected complete acceptance. He was strong and stubborn, factors that could be used to his advantage if she could manage to focus his energies on her therapy techniques.

She laid aside the appointment book and concentrated fully on his first lesson. "This is a crash course," she said. "Though stuttering is seldom caused by an actual physical obstruction, the methods I prefer are based on a trained muscle response. Typically, when a dysfluent person is faced with a stressful situation, the larynx constricts causing the vocal cords to close. Trying to force air through the larynx results in a pressure that causes the stutter."

He unbent slightly and leaned forward in his chair. "How can you exercise the larynx?"

"Not by lifting weights with your tongue," she said, hoping to relieve the tension she felt building. "Here's an example. You can stop your breathing when you are under water, and you can control breath patterns when you swim."

She was aware that he was intently watching the rise and fall of her breasts as she showed him the exaggerated inhalation and exhalation method, and she fought the urge to chastely fold her arms over her chest. Reminding herself that he was a client—not in-

terested in her body, but her therapeutic expertise—
she continued. "Most of the time, however, you don't
need to think about taking a breath. It's a natural, involuntary process."

"I understand," he said, lifting his gaze to her eyes.

If Crystal had not learned her therapy instructions
by rote, she would have been too flustered to proceed.
His cobalt-blue eyes hypnotized her and seemed to be
sending messages that stirred impulses she had thought
were safely dormant. A certain intimacy was necessary
in this instructor-student relationship, but she had
never before felt the closeness so sensually. Her voice
was stilted as she uttered the familiar phrases. "The
idea is not to attempt to force an involuntary muscle,
but to relax the larynx. This is accomplished by breathing before speaking. You expel a small gasp of air and
then talk freely."

She illustrated by exhaling loudly and saying, "Good
afternoon, Mr. Todhunter. How nice to see you."

"Sounds good on you," he said. "Breathy. Like
Marilyn Monroe. But it's not my style. I think I'd
rather stutter."

A broad smile lighted her face. "Do you realize
what just happened? You said the word stutter for the
first time since you came into this house."

"I did?" His eyebrows lifted in surprise. His accomplishment caught him unprepared. "I did. I said
it. How did that happen? I wasn't doing any special
breathing."

"You're relaxing." Significantly she added, "And
you're beginning to trust me."

Crystal's enthusiasm was tempered by the realization that Luke's ability to relax indicated a new level of

trust. He was beginning to accept her as his therapist,
to believe she could help him. Apparently, she thought
with ironic disappointment, he didn't feel the same
tension that rose urgently within her. While she was
developing an acute case of jitters, he was unwinding,
feeling safe in her presence.

That was as it should be, she reminded herself
sternly. This one-sided infatuation had to stop. It
should never be a part of therapist-client procedures.
At least all the textbooks advised against it. Crystal
shook her head in an attempt to clear out all these
unprofessional thoughts. She would have to guard
against her natural inclinations where Luke Todhunter was concerned. She submerged her feelings
under a cheery, encouraging smile and used her best
clinical manner. "Now try the air-flow technique."

He inhaled. "The rain in Spain stays—"

"No. You exhale...like a sigh. And please spare me
the Henry Higgins rhetoric. Use your opening remarks for your town meeting."

"Where did you get this method?"

"It was perfected by Dr. Martin Schwartz, and I
was fortunate enough to be tutored by Dr. Schwartz
himself. I combine his air-flow technique with the
philosophies of Dr. Sheehan of the Rollins Institute
who recommends a psychological acceptance of stuttering. That's the sort of work I'm doing with my
dysfluent speakers group. Now, try the air flow
again."

He took a deep breath, filling his chest cavity. He
spoke on the exhalation. "Good evening." He breathed
again. "The people of Jefferson County." Another
breath. "Have a great deal to be proud of. How's that?"

"Very nice," she congratulated. Her compliment

had double meaning. It was her turn to stare at his chest, and she very much approved. "Try it again. This time make the breathing less obvious."

With each repetition, the words circulated more evenly and his gasp became less apparent. "You're a quick study, Luke. Now make the air flow invisible." She illustrated.

"You didn't breathe," he accused.

"Yes I did. But it was completely unnoticeable, exactly the way you will learn to do it. I want to show you that you don't have to replace the stutter with a different habit. As you pointed out, it would be just as obtrusive for you to hyperventilate during your town meeting."

She repeated the exercise.

He shook his head. 'I'm sure you didn't breathe."

"Come here, Luke. Put your hand in front of my lips."

He hovered by her chair, leaning close. One large, leathery hand poised barely a centimeter away from her mouth. She could smell his nearness, a faint, masculine aroma. The intent light from his eyes matched her own glazed stare as he held the intimate pose rigidly.

Her own fingers were tightly clasped in her lap to avoid accidentally touching him. The warmth from their bodies mingled, and the air around them felt as sultry and moist as a tropical rain forest. A droplet of perspiration trickled between her breasts as she concentrated on her breath control. "Good evening, people of Jefferson County. You should be proud."

"I still didn't feel anything."

"You did, too. I was performing the exercise correctly."

Silently she pleaded with her senses, ordering her knees to stop trembling.

"Try it again, Crystal."

"Good evening, people of...."

She paused, stopping the air flow, stopping her pulse, stopping the pretense that she would be satisfied with a platonic friendship. She couldn't deny it—she was drawn to him by a compelling velocity, powerful as a tidal wave, a whirlpool that thundered in her ears and drowned her objectivity in a sea of womanly longing.

The warm blue of his eyes fascinated her. His lips, slightly parted, formed the most exquisite of destinations. Like an exhausted swimmer going down for the third time, her life telescoped before her.

Yet, Crystal was a survivor. She fought the ecstasy of surrender.

Her paralysis lasted only an instant though it seemed like eternity. She broke the magnetic spell by clearing her throat and slouching back in the chair. "Did you feel it?" she asked.

"Yes, Crystal. I felt it."

She turned her head toward the west windows. Evening shadows had fallen, and the darkness frightened her. Turn into a pumpkin? She mocked herself. *Not this time, Cinderella.*

There would be no midnights in his arms, no glass slippers nor happily ever afters. For they were contemporary people, and he had consulted her on a professional level. She was wrong to believe, even for a moment, in fairy tales.

3

CAUTION WAS HER BYWORD for therapy sessions with Luke. She carefully phrased her expert instructions and teased him like a buddy, but she was always alert. As soon as she felt her attraction for him rising, she prudently danced away. Caution. Like a moth to a flame, she was irresistibly fascinated, but managed to always escape without singeing her wings.

They met in her office every morning at eight, and she discovered the importance of hot, black coffee to their daybreak mood. Though she was not a morning person, the early sessions were far less difficult than the five-to-seven shift. During the 8:00 A.M. therapy, Luke was serious and hardworking. By late afternoon, his diligence had slipped and a playful sense of humor emerged. Night after night, he asked for a date. Her consistent refusal became a standing joke.

On Saturday evening Luke appeared in full, formal regalia, wearing a black tuxedo with velvet lapels and a ruffled white shirt. The precise tailoring emphasized his lean, muscular physique. He consulted a heavy gold wristwatch. "It's five o'clock. If you start right now, you could be dressed for the first curtain at eight."

"It wouldn't take me three hours to get ready." Though his suave appearance took her breath away,

Crystal maintained her caution. "That is, if I were going anywhere."

"It's a special fund-raiser for the Colorado Ballet. They're doing *Firebird*, and I have sixth row center seats."

"Enjoy yourself."

"Since you're such a speedy dresser, we could go out for dinner first. Maybe to the Fairmont."

She was tempted, but wise enough to know that the combination of *Firebird*, Fairmont and formal dress could be lethal to her already dwindling self-control. Involvement. Commitment. She had no time for those, especially not with a client.

Determinedly, she marched toward her office. "I thought we would use the videotape tonight. We'll record your speech and then play it back." She paused in the doorway. "It's rather nice that you dressed for the occasion."

"May I use the telephone. I hate to waste this seat."

"Certainly. I'll set up the camera."

It took him approximately three minutes to make another date. Perversely, that fact disturbed Crystal. She imagined a string of panting admirers, all of them ready to cancel their plans on a moment's notice. What would her position be in that pecking order? None, she told herself firmly.

"How do we start?" he asked.

"You stand behind the podium." She gestured to the portable lectern that resided in a corner of her office when not in use.

"I'm glad we're doing something different," he said. "I was really getting bored with all the air-flow repetitions."

"That is something you'll learn to live with. Only

through constant reinforcement will the air flow become second nature. You should practice every day of your life."

She ignored his grimace and continued. "It's really difficult to treat you, Luke. Do you realize that I've never heard you stutter?"

"Thank God."

"Anyway, I'm going to work with you on presentation—typical exercises to improve your public-speaking abilities."

She outlined their agenda: videotaping his speech, viewing the results and critiquing, then a second videotape to note the improvements.

The first taping was impressive. Crystal wondered if her own attraction to him colored her opinion and decided objectively that anyone would call him eloquent. He projected a strong sincerity and warm charisma.

"You're a wonderful speaker," she enthused. "I was going to lecture you about eye contact and resonance and gesture, but you're a natural. I can understand why you went into law. You must be dynamite with a jury."

"I've never made a courtroom presentation. I'm the guy in the back room with the law books and the briefs. But I've always admired Perry Mason."

She pulled her eyebrows in an exaggerated scowl and took on the Perry Mason role. "Isn't it true, Mr. Suspect, that you prefer your steaks well done? And what were you doing with that chain saw on the night of the murder?"

"That's the moment when Paul Drake, Mason's assistant, comes scampering into the room with vital info." His shoulders rose and fell in a self-effacing shrug. "That's my job."

"Then let's trade roles. I'd rather be Della Street, anyway. You be the brilliant attorney."

He hitched his thumbs in his velvet lapels and sternly addressed Rorschach the cat who sauntered nonchalantly through the office. "I've just received notice, Mr. Rorschach, that your scratching post was found near the scene of the crime, and I submit that you knew the precise location of the rat's body because you left it there yourself."

Rorschach mewed plaintively.

"That cat is guilty," Crystal proclaimed.

"Wrong. It's always the least likely person. You, Della Street, with your auburn hair and amber eyes—you have perpetrated crimes beyond your knowledge. Your mere presence has driven better men than I to deeds of passion." He strode toward her, masterfully holding forth in a deep, melodious voice that she found extremely seductive even in playacting. "For your punishment, you are hereby sentenced to an evening at the ballet."

"You've already got a date."

"I'll break it."

"If I may say so—with great conviction—that sort of behavior is indefensible. You're obviously toying with a woman's affections."

"I'm a cad," he agreed. "But my sister won't mind. She'll be delighted that I've finally found someone who will go out with me."

Crystal turned away and fiddled with her camera so he wouldn't notice the Cheshire cat grin that spread from ear to ear on her gamine face. His sister was his date. Why should she find that so gratifying? "Be sure you're home early tonight and well rested," she advised. "I have a special assignment for you tomorrow."

"Let me guess. I get to read *War and Peace* aloud using the air-flow technique."

"Meet me at two o'clock in front of Carberry's on Colfax."

"CARBERRY SHOPPERS.... Attention. We have a special in the Home Products Department. Twenty-four one pound boxes of low-suds biodegradable detergent, our name brand, are reduced to half price."

Crystal had arranged this unusual public speaking engagement with a former student who now managed Carberry's. For one hour, Luke made announcements on the store's PA system.

"May I have your attention, please. We have a lost boy answering to the name Michael. He is wearing brown shorts and a red Snoopy T-shirt. Would Michael's mother please come to Customer Service."

Luke spoke without a trace of dysfluency. The only problem came with the surfacing of his sense of the ridiculous. "For the next five minutes only, we have rubber baby buggy bumpers on special. Attention. We sell seashells from the seashore. Get 'em while they last."

Crystal thanked the store manager profusely and hustled the future politician out into the sun. "What was that all about?"

He made a megaphone around his lips. "Attention, shoppers. Get your red-hot larynx here, only slightly used by a former stutterer."

"I will forgive you only because I understand your excitement over a job well done. Do you realize that you just performed for an audience of over one hundred people?"

"Attention, speech therapist. It's not hard when I don't see their faces." His voice dropped to conversational level. "How about a picnic in the mountains?"

In spite of her firm resolutions, she chuckled. "How could I refuse such a romantically phrased proposition?"

"You mean you'll accept? After five days of constant invitations, you are finally going to relent?"

"Of course not."

"But you just said you would."

"I said, how could I refuse? Pay attention, now. This is how I refuse: no way, Todhunter."

"Then, can I buy you an ice-cream cone?" he asked. "I promise not to make lewd and suggestive passes at you over the Chocolate Marble Surprise."

An ice-cream parlor seemed safe enough, and they strolled across the parking lot toward a candy-striped shop. He ordered three scoops, all different flavors, to her one, and they sat opposite each other in a hot-pink booth. She carefully arranged her knees to avoid accidentally bumping him.

"You can tell a lot about people from watching them eat ice cream," he said.

"Such as?"

"Take a look at that little girl over there. She's timing her licks to make that cone last twenty minutes. See how she's gloating. Her friend is already done."

"Which proves?"

"Some people take their pleasures slowly, savoring every mouthful. Others gobble them up and are ready for more."

"Very interesting," she commented, taking a nibble

of Cherry Custard Sunrise and letting it melt on her tongue. "What would you deduce about someone who orders a cone that looks like a tricolored Tower of Pisa?"

"Obviously the glutton type," he admitted with a slurp at the Licorice Swirl. "Somebody who sees what he wants and goes after it."

"Shall we talk about tomorrow night? Your speaking engagement before my DSD group?" She pulled out her "caution" attitude and waved it like a flag. Their conversation had begun to border on personal, and that direction was taboo. "Do you think you're ready, Luke?"

"Absolutely not. I'm scared as hell." He cheerfully attacked the middle dip of Blueberry Hill. "What time is this close encounter set for?"

"Seven sharp."

"If I picked you up at five, we'd have time for dinner. A little wine, a little lobster. Maybe we'd forget entirely about the DSD meeting."

"You know my answer." Though she was secretly pleased at his persistent offers, she doubted the sincerity of his courtship. "Why do you keep asking, Luke? I've explained several times that it is not appropriate for me to see you on a social basis while you are under such intensive treatment."

"I'm a champion of lost causes, remember?"

"If I actually said yes, I bet you'd back out." She figured that his game was pursuit, and her refusals intrigued him. He probably never before encountered a woman who could resist those gorgeous blue eyes and the boyish lock of blond hair that just begged to be pushed back from his forehead. "I ought to agree, just to see you turn tail and run."

"Try me."

A yellow light blinked behind her eyes. *Caution. Caution. Emotional well-being in danger.* "I wouldn't give you the satisfaction."

THE FOLLOWING AFTERNOON, their session proceeded as usual with Luke practicing his speech using the airflow technique. He spoke before a mirror, into a microphone and over a tape recorder.

Crystal sat quietly in the large wingback chair with her feet tucked up under her full, turquoise skirt. She usually dressed more formally for the DSD meeting, but the extreme August heat dictated a more comfortable, cotton outfit—a soft, white peasant blouse and Indian-style skirt with a silver Navajo belt.

She recognized a degree of tension in her prize pupil and tried to keep him busy so his mind would not wander into apprehension about the impending speech. "Now I want you to purposely stutter."

"Again?" he said impatiently.

"And again. And again."

"C-c-can we d-d-dare to d-dream of a b-better C-colorado?"

"Stop. Repeat without the stutter."

He did so, precisely.

"I think you're ready, Luke. Your vocal control is really very good."

"Does that mean I'm cured?"

"This is not an either/or proposition, as you well know. Speech dysfluency is unpredictable. Someone who has always spoken perfectly might suddenly begin to stutter. Another habitual stutterer might—without any apparent reason—stop. There are no rules, only exceptions."

"And no cure," he added listlessly.

"It's all behavioral. Never trust a person who claims to have a cure." She realized that this lecture was not the best morale booster and modified her tone. "No one can really predict what constitutes successful therapy for stuttering. Hypnotism. Behavior modification. Several therapists swear by a process of substitution."

"Tell me about substitution. What does that mean?" He meandered about the room without apparent direction, pausing at her desk to straighten a pen set, adjusting the knot of his necktie using a silver vase for a mirror, flicking invisible specks of lint from his navy-blue suit.

Crystal noticed that he seemed distracted, unable to concentrate. She wished for a magic remedy for his indifference. There must be some method to infuse him with a positive, alert attitude. If only she were free to comfort him with more than bland, intellectual salvos. "It's generally recognized that blockage is most likely to occur in the initial speaking. Once that first hurdle is passed—the first sentence uttered with fluency—the rest isn't nearly so tough." Her voice sounded hollow and dull. Couldn't he perceive the concern behind her words? She forced a smile. "One form of substitution is snapping the fingers."

"Every time you feel a stutter coming on, you snap?" He strolled the length of her office. There were folding chairs for the DSD group, five chairs facing the lectern. Her video camera was set up to the rear. Luke avoided the speaker's position with measured strides.

When Crystal snapped her fingers, he turned sharply. "That's a little weird, therapist lady."

"I agree, but if it works, who cares? They can use a slap on the thigh, or a wink, or anything."

"Anything?"

"I might have known that your dirty mind would find a way to corrupt my scholarly explanation," she teased, hoping to stimulate a spirited response.

"Actually, I'm serious. Would any gesture be effective as a substitute for stuttering? Isn't the air-flow method of speaking a form of that therapy?"

"The air-flow methods deal specifically with the problem of tightening in the larynx. But any programmed signal that served to divert the stutterer's attention and allowed the vocal cords to relax would make normal speech possible." Again, she made an effort to be cheerful. "You could chatter your teeth or wiggle your toes or pat your tummy."

Abruptly, his attention focused, and Crystal was the target of his strange, predatory scrutiny. Luke's pacing halted. He stood perfectly still. Crystal had the distinct impression that a trap was being laid, and that she had already risen to the bait.

Five days ago, she wouldn't have understood all the nuances of Luke's behavior—the quirk of his eyebrow, the forward thrust of his jaw and the taut set of his shoulders. She would have interpreted his stance as aggressive. But by now she had learned the depth of his sensitivity, and knew that his intention was not to intimidate or frighten her. That realization made his intensity all the more fearful. As he stalked toward her with pantherlike grace, she sensed in the pit of her churning stomach what was to happen next.

"Would a kiss be acceptable substitution behavior?" he asked.

"I don't believe it has been tested." She clung desperately to her standard flippancy. "But if you feel the need to kiss your hand before speaking, go right ahead."

He held the back of his hand to his lips and dropped it quickly. "Not so good. Why don't I try it with you?"

He bent from the waist and seized her wrist, slowly raising her hand to his lips in courtly gesture. His attitude was chaste and polite, waiting for the signal from her.

When no protest stilled his tender advances, he lifted the other hand to join its mate and clasped the slender fingers in his calloused, but gentle, grip. "Crystal, you're trembling."

Her lips formed a reply that was never spoken, and all of her caution vanished in the quiet sweep of a summer breeze that tantalized the curtains on her open windows. Her objectivity was gone. Competent self-control melted. She was defenseless as a bunny in a snare, an utterly willing prey to the sensual magic in his sky-blue eyes.

He tugged slightly, and her response was instinctive. She glided to her feet. Her head tilted back, and lips parted to meet his kiss. The feather-light touch on her mouth was reverential, and the texture was more tenderly eloquent than anything she had ever experienced.

Her hands mounted the strong sinews of his forearms and rested on the hard planes of his chest. The feel of his body fulfilled her intemperate yearnings, and her appetite grew stronger as she fed on the lingering taste of his lips, soft as first dew on summer flowers. She moaned as his tongue worshipped the satin flesh inside her mouth. Blossoming and awak-

ening, she drew succor from him as a starving nest-
ling might be appeased and comforted by its parents.

Luke gathered her into his arms, fusing her body
with his own. His strength grew fierce as their kiss
prolonged. He crushed her against him and gently released, then held her close again. Their heartbeats
echoed in a single, wildly accelerating rhythm.

He seemed gigantic, as though he could completely
envelop her. Yet they fit together perfectly. Their idyl-
lic embrace could have been sculpted from one living
stone as his lean, hard body molded to her slender
contours.

A small, nagging inner voice told her that the bliss-
ful, savored moment had to end. She could not allow
herself the pleasure of consummation. There was her
reputation as a therapist to consider, her goals, her
prized independence. She forced her lips from his and
made an effort at resistance. "Luke," she gasped.
"Please stop."

He murmured an unintelligible response and freed
one of his hands to explore the angles of her body.
With infinite delicacy, he stroked her slender neck
and the slope of her shoulders. His hand found and
began fondling the tight bud of her swollen breast.
She inhaled sharply. How could such ecstasy be
wrong? Yet, she protested verbally even as her body
clove more tightly to him. "Let me go."

A surge of panic swept through her. Her skin felt as
though she'd been flayed to the heightened sensitivity
of an open wound. She burned for him, and the
power of her longing terrified her. This was not the
safe realm of fantasy, but an earthy, aching reality.

"Let me go, Luke. Damn it, I'll scream."

She wedged her fists between them, feeling him,

adoring him, yet pushing him away. She burst free and confronted him.

Confusion was written on his face. And pain.

"What happened?" she demanded. An angry, red flush mottled her neck. She brushed vigorously at her full skirt, seeking order and composure in the turquoise folds. With one ragged breath after another, she willed her heart to stop its fluttering palpitations. "Answer me, Luke. Don't you dare play the strong silent type."

He regarded her stoically, as the reality of rejection asserted its hold upon him and the light died in his eyes. His stillborn desire for her lay crushed by disappointment. She didn't want him. All her refusals had been real. He had mistaken her kindness for something more, something special. Trust. Would he never learn the boundaries of trust?

His shoulders stiffened. His features were set in granite, rock hard as the mountains he dearly loved. The tightness in Luke's throat reminded him that speaking would be hopeless. Without a word, he strode to the door.

"L-l-luke," cried Crystal in a pressured stutter that filled the air with its guttural echo. "Y-y-you c-c-can't leave."

He turned slowly. Bright tears glittered in his eyes as he looked down at the quaking form of Crystal Baxter, speech therapist. "You?" he said.

The last rays of sunset through the west windows glinted red fire in her auburn hair. Her chin was raised defiantly. "Y-y-yes, Luke. I stutter, t-t-too."

He approached her eagerly, his arms outstretched to take her burden from her, to release the agony he knew so well. He wanted to hold and to comfort her, to quell the demon that tortured her lovely amber eyes. A strong emotion rushed through him. For the first time, he'd found a woman who could share completely in his fears and his triumphs. With her by his side, Luke could conquer the world.

She held up her hands. "D-d-don't touch me."

"You're not a leper. Besides, you can't infect me. I've already got the disease."

"I won't have it, Luke. I won't have us c-c-clinging together like shipwreck victims waiting to be rescued."

"Then, why did you call me back?"

"I c-c-can help you," she asserted. "It's not fair to deny you my help."

Crystal forced herself to conquer her vulnerability. She had not come this far from stuttering to establish a relationship based on her handicap. If she was meant to be with Luke Todhunter, their mating must be based on victory, not shared weakness.

"Why didn't you tell me?" he asked.

"Would you have believed me?" she challenged, once more in control of her irregular breathing. "Or would have have assumed that I was using a therapist's trick to gain your confidence."

She saw in his expression the confirmation to her question. She knew her stutterers only too well.

"Unlike your experience, I received excellent therapy for my stutter," she revealed. "But it continued to resurface—in times of stress—until I was treated by Dr. Schwartz. I studied the phenomenon, and my studies became my vocation. So, you see, I have a unique qualification as a speech therapist, one that I choose not to advertise."

She didn't feel that she was reaching him. His grin

was too broad, and he was staring at her like he'd just won the lottery. What was he thinking? An edge of anger crept into her voice. "I regret this interruption in your therapy, Luke. In the future, I will attempt to be more controlled."

"Don't apologize."

"Don't you understand? My work is the most important thing in my life. The only thing. Neither you nor anyone else will compromise my goals." She returned to her chair. Her cool mask slid into place. "Please be seated, Luke. We have a lot of work to do before that town meeting on Friday."

"I don't care about the town meeting. I never wanted to be a politician, anyway." His blue eyes shone eagerly. "I want to talk about us. There's a chemistry that you can't ignore. Don't be so hard, Crystal. Be like amber for me, glowing and warm."

His words created a jumble of conflicting emotions within her. She could not refute his description—a chemical reaction. That powerful interaction had started from the moment she spied his handsome profile through the glass oval in her front door, and it grew more potent daily with their shared experiences.

Yet, the joy she should have felt was marred by fear and anger. She was Crystal, with a vision as pure and clear as her name. Her life was well-ordered, though hectic, and her goal was clearly defined. If she succumbed to this attraction, her destiny would never be the same. For these five days, she had fought to control herself. Where had she gone off course? How had he managed with one embrace to eclipse the distant star that had led her onward?

In his smile, she saw the promise of a new future, tender and sweet as a fairy tale. But what would happen to all her carefully laid plans? Her father always said that only red ants make plans for the winter. Was she being petty and mean spirited? No, she told herself. She had spent her lifetime pursuing very real truths and ambitions, and she would not abandon her commitments for the pleasure of Luke's kiss.

"Perhaps it would be better, Luke, if you found another therapist."

"I'll take my chances." His grin displayed even, white teeth against his tanned face. "You won't get rid of me that easily."

"But your therapy is important, and I've compromised my ability to treat you."

"Damn the treatments and the air flow and the stutter. There's only one thing on my mind, Amber Lady."

"No. You came to me as a client. That was the only relationship I ever considered between us. Now, we can't even pretend to continue in therapy. It would be for the best if you left right now."

"Are you refusing to help me?" he asked slyly. "You know how hard it was for me to ask for therapy. You know I'll never ask again."

"But you're so close. Someone else can see you through this town meeting."

"I won't go to anyone else. You, of all people, should understand." His serious expression emphasized the gravity of his explanation. For once, Luke was not teasing or joking. "I am a stutterer, Crystal, and there's no one else I will trust. You are my therapist."

Luke's argument, despite Crystal's slipping emotional equilibrium, made too much sense. His trust had not been given lightly, and their special relationship—though devastating—boded well for the treatment of his impediment. Why should he suffer because she had lost her self-control?

"Look at me, Crystal. I'm about to speak before a group. You can't abandon me now."

She was convinced. It would be irresponsible to drop him as a client at this important juncture. She had to see him through. "All right, Luke. You offer me no choice."

"I'm not being fair, am I? But I never claimed to be above playing on your sympathies."

"My sympathies?" she rejoined spiritedly. "Compassion is the last thing I feel for you. My interest is absolutely clinical. Untouched by human emotion."

What a lie! It was fortunate that they were not in the realm of fairy tales because her nose would have pinocchioed to three feet long. "I see you as a challenge, Todhunter."

"You won't be disappointed. Bring on your groups and your videotapes and your air-flow techniques. If the only way I can see you is for speech therapy, I'm ready."

The doorbell signaled the arrival of the first member of DSD, Dysfluent Speakers of Denver.

4

THE FIRST SOFT GLOW OF DAWN illuminated the primrose-and-gray paisley print of the wallpaper in her office. The wakening song of robins mingled with early traffic rumbles on a night-cooled August breeze whispering through the open west windows. Crystal wrapped her teal-blue kimono tightly across her bare breasts and shivered. It was the loneliest time of the day, the hour when her empty bed felt cold and hard.

She had left that bed over an hour ago, unable to sleep. An uncomfortable tension had intruded on her slumber, and the virile presence of Luke Todhunter had dominated her dreams. The unbidden remembrance of his kiss had roused her, and she had given up on sleep.

Now Crystal sought the familiar solace of work and came to her office prepared to exorcise the memory of him. Yet in the office his essence was strongest. The folding chairs were neatly returned to the closet, but the lectern reminded her; Luke had stood here. She sat in the wingback chair; Luke had kissed her here. The very walls—papered by Luke—echoed his resonant baritone. The nap of the carpet bore his footprint.

With a decisive flick of the wrist, she banished him. "Go haunt somebody else," she commanded. "Somebody with more time."

Thus resolved, she positioned herself at her desk

and resumed her work where she'd left off yesterday—with a new recitation of sonnets from the Texas minister. She plugged in the cassette and began listening but her mind wandered. Was that a slur? She rewound the tape slightly.

"'Presume not on thy heart when mine is slain—'" she skipped ahead "'—the perfect ceremony of love's rite....'"

"Be quiet, Reverend." She turned off the tape, regretting this choice of lesson. Every other word focused on love.

Crystal eyed the videotape recorder. Luke's performance at the DSD meeting was set for replay. Should she give in to the temptation? Maybe seeing him on tape would make his memory less potent, she rationalized. She tapped her pencil on the wide oak top of the desk. Was it a weakness to succumb? Or merely curiosity?

Ironically, this moment had been predicted by Ginger MacKay, the first arrival at the DSD meeting. Crystal and Ginger had enjoyed a long-standing friendship, having met years before when they were the only two women at a lecture on stuttering. Crystal was always buoyed by her friend's vivacious nonsense. Last night had been the exception when Ginger had taken her aside and whispered, "He's a Libra, isn't he? Just l-l-like you."

"I have no idea."

"Take my word for it. You match beautifully." Ginger loved to foretell the future. Tarot cards and horoscopes and numerology were all part of her repertoire. "You're both kind of stubborn, and it won't be all smooth sailing, but I know you'll work it out. Oh, Crystal, I'm so happy for you."

"Would you like some fresh tea leaves so you can confirm the wedding date? Or would coffee grounds do?" Crystal glared at the short, raven-haired woman whose dark eyes glittered mischievously. "Honestly, Ginger. He's only a client."

"Don't tell me you're not attracted to him. With those broad shoulders and Paul Newman eyes. He's a real honey. A hunk, as my teenage daughter would say." She sighed dramatically. "If only I wasn't married."

"More coffee?"

"And the way he looks at you. Like you're some kind of goddess."

"Stop it, Ginger."

"Well? Aren't you attracted to him?"

"I haven't given it much thought."

"You don't need to think, Crystal," she said with an exasperated gesture that set the bangles on her arm to clanging. "Just let yourself go with the flow."

Throughout the therapy meeting her self-styled gypsy friend had flashed meaningful winks at her. Ginger's parting comment was, "I'll bet you spend half the night replaying a certain videotape of a certain Libra man."

"Good night, Ginger," Crystal had said firmly as she palmed that devastating Libran off on her friend. "Luke will walk you to your car."

"Best offer I've had in years. Don't tell Charlie." She waved gaily. "Sweet dreams, Crystal."

As she watched Ginger and Luke stroll beyond the circle of her porch lamp, Crystal had wished for nothing more than the pure release of dreamless slumber. Yet, such peace was not to be. Crystal had tossed fitfully until she finally gave in to Ginger's prophecy.

Using the remote control, Crystal started the video-tape.

The VCR unit on her television fuzzed to life. The first images were out of focus because the camera had jostled in her hand when she had adjusted the tripod to accommodate Luke's height. Then, in living color, he appeared. His eyebrows lifted quizzically. His slight smile was engaging. Even on videotape, the brilliant blue of his eyes was startling. As Ginger had remarked, Luke Todhunter—Libra or not—was a real honey of a hunk.

She heard her own disembodied voice saying, "All right, Luke. The camera is set. Whenever you're ready."

Another off-camera rejoinder came from Mr. Pappas, who always found it necessary to repeat everything Crystal said. His comment was shushed by Dr. Ince, whose dislike for the Pappas parrot was no surprise to the other three members of the group.

Ginger's giggle was clearly recorded, then the audio portion of the tape went silent. Luke gave every appearance of ease. Though Crystal knew his poise came from an iron-willed control, he managed to convey a casual image. He would make a compelling politician, she thought, able to cruise to victory without ever opening his mouth. His rugged blondness alone would have the female population of Jefferson County beating down the doors of their polling places to cast votes for Luke Todhunter.

How quietly he stood! His chest rose and fell using the air-flow technique. During the first half-hour of their meeting, Crystal had instructed the group to practice with him. The exercise had served to reinforce their own habits and to minimize the tension caused by a newcomer. When Luke was comfortable with the exercise, she had offered him escape from this particular type of public speaking. His refusal had been emphatic.

"Good evening," said the tall figure at the podium.

Her pride at his successful enunciation of the difficult "g" sound was erased with his next utterance.

"P-p-people of Jefferson C-c-county...."

He stopped speaking, and she willed her breath into his throat. His grip on the oak lectern was white knuckled. His mouth contorted with the effort. He took a deep breath. "People of Jefferson County. You have many reasons to be p-p-proud. Your schools. Your p-p-parks. Your p-p-pioneering spirit of independence. Y-y-your...."

He hammered his fist on the podium with a force she feared would splinter the wood.

She saw herself appear on the screen. "Thank you, Mr. Todhunter."

Her disappointment was evident as she watched the tape. She remembered cursing her judgment. The last thing Luke needed was an unsuccessful effort. She should have known better. This failure would reinforce his fears, raise his stress level at his next attempt and therefore make the stutter almost inevitable.

She saw herself gesture toward a seat, excusing him from his painfully blocked speech. She had not anticipated his next move.

He clutched her forearm and turned her to face him. She could still feel the force of his powerful grasp. Intense determination burned through deep blue eyes that stood out in stark relief against his face which had paled beneath its tan. "I'm n-n-not f-finished."

"All right, Luke. Let's practice the air flow. Breathe in. Exhale. That's correct. Allow the air to relax the larynx."

She had laid her hand on his throat as though she could physically remove the obstruction. He was so much taller than she. Standing on tiptoe and concentrating on his throat and lips, she had to tilt her head back.

On the tape, she saw herself blush. Here was irrefutable evidence of her desire. Her lips parted slightly as she illustrated the breathing technique. She recognized in her unconsciously arched back a womanly invitation. Could she blame him for what happened next?

His arms encircled her. In slow motion, his lips sought hers. She saw herself being thoroughly kissed and heard the roar of approval from Dr. Ince. "Go to it, boy. I've wanted to do that myself."

That instant captured on tape had marked the nadir of her career, the lowest point of her professionalism. The situation had catapulted beyond her control and demolished the careful image she'd constructed. She remembered the constricting of her own throat and how she had dared not speak for fear that her own stutter would appear.

Yet the film image was contrary to the turmoil she recalled. That Crystal on the television screen owned bright, gold-flecked eyes. Her traitorous lips were smiling. She seemed to be a happy, complacent woman as he took her firmly by both arms and placed her beyond the camera's range.

Luke Todhunter, the politician, stepped back to the podium. He cleared his throat once and began to speak. "People of Jefferson County. You have reason to be proud. Your school system is exemplary, ranked number three in the nation. Your parks are well-planned and beautiful. Your pioneering spirit brings memories of the founders of this magnificent county. I commend this pride and urge you to be true to your roots. Together we will save the mountain heritage of our community. We will stand firm in the face of opposition. We will defeat Coyote Creek Dam."

Not a trace of a stutter betrayed him as he continued. His eloquent arguments piled one on top of another. That low-key baritone radiated confidence and leadership.

Crystal hadn't heard his words. As she stood by his side, she only remembered a buzzing confusion and a sense that the roof might at any moment cave in on her.

He had conquered his stutter, and his success validated her therapy techniques. Or did it? She ruefully imagined a professional paper on the effects of kissing your clients. Such ludicrous documentation would be rife with examples of turning frogs into princes and the value of mouth-to-mouth resuscitation. She would title it "Sex and the Single Stutterer."

On the tape, Luke finished his prepared remarks and asked for questions from the audience.

Dr. Ince asked, "How do I sign up for the kind of therapy you're getting from Ms Baxter?"

"I'm sorry, sir. That's a professional secret."

"What profession?"

Crystal recognized the tiny flame of anger that caused a tightening in Luke's stubborn jaw and rationalized that it was good practice for him to deal with obnoxious questions from this small audience. Even if the teasing came at her expense.

"As I am sure you know, Dr. Ince," Luke replied steadily, "the relationship between therapist and client is confidential. However, I do assure you that Ms Baxter had no knowledge of my intentions. I sincerely hope she will not be embarrassed by inquiries such as yours and will find it in her heart to forgive me."

Crystal asked for other questions.

"Any more questions?" Mr. Pappas echoed.

The rest of the group joined in the spirit of the exercise, asking intelligent questions about the dam and acting like an alternately hostile and supportive audience. Ginger was the most vocal. She agreed wholeheartedly with Luke's position and, in her eagerness to defend him, stammered several times. Crystal did not correct her. The purpose of this therapy group was to encourage these stutterers to accept their handicaps and to realize that occasional missteps need not signal total relapses.

When Luke had satisfied all their discussion with intelligent competence, he raised his hand to indicate an end to his speech. The group applauded.

Her videotape faded to blank static, and Crystal reversed the images until she reached their kiss. She froze the picture.

"Some therapist," she said aloud. "My Lord, I'm drooling all over him. This whole thing is my fault."

The dawn solitude offered no reply. There was quiet confirmation in the instant replay of a tall, lean man embracing a slender, auburn-haired lady whose fingers rested lightly on his shoulders and whose lips accepted his willingly.

Crystal wasted very little time in introspection. She preferred action, and her solution to this situation was obvious and immediate. Professionals do not fawn over their clients. This relationship had to be changed.

The image on the video screen mocked her decision. *That* Crystal Baxter with the delicate wisps of hair escaping her neat twist could not dismiss him so easily. *That* woman fantasized about romance and wanted nothing more than to collapse into Luke's waiting arms. *That* Crystal loved to be called Amber. Her lips longed to be swollen with his kisses. She ached with emptiness and unfulfilled desires.

The other Crystal, a pragmatic therapist, distrusted that sensual creature with the overactive imagination. Where would she lead? What were her purposes? Her infatuations were uncontrolled, unpredictable and instinctive.

The sensible Crystal turned off the videotape with a resounding click. This travesty of therapy should not be allowed to continue. Her reactions to Luke were destroying her hard-won credibility. She ought to refer him to a colleague.

She padded barefoot into the kitchen to make coffee and to consider possible referrals. Another woman therapist who espoused similar treatment was swiftly rejected. "Too blond," Crystal decided unprofessionally. "And too busty. What Luke needs is a nice, older man."

The kissable side of her personality added, *what Crystal needs is Luke.*

"No," she said, pounding a delicate fist on the kitchen counter. She hadn't the time to devote to an affair. "Not now when I'm so close."

The place on her newly papered wall had already been selected for hanging her Ph.D. diploma. She simply couldn't deviate from her chosen path to indulge in a romantic interlude.

You could have both, said the nagging voice. *Lots of women combine love and career.*

She stilled that objection with a review of her busy schedule. It wouldn't be fair to him, she thought, and he probably wouldn't understand. Why should such a gorgeous hunk of man wait patiently in second-place while she devoted herself to her overwhelming professional responsibilities?

It was better to call a halt to this kissing while she still had some self-control. Her father would have said a finger in the dike sometimes stops the flood.

She had to patch her vulnerability with tons of concrete. As dawn became morning, she resolved to be stern and steady and competent. Her life would not be disrupted. As if to affirm that decision, she returned to her daily routine and went in search of her morning newspaper.

Rorschach greeted her at the front door, mewing loudly to warn her of the unusual deliveryman who sat on the porch swing reading the editorial page. "Good morning, Amber Lady."

She stepped back, stunned. "What are you doing here, Luke?"

"Taking a survey on the normal wake-up time for speech pathologists. You're earlier than most."

She noticed his casual outfit of worn Levi's and an open-necked cotton shirt of crimson plaid. "Why are you dressed like that? Is there a lawyer's holiday that I don't know about?"

"We are going to the mountains. I knew you were unconvinced by my eloquent arguments last night, so

I decided you should see the site for Coyote Creek Dam.''

This was exactly the sort of interruption she had feared. Her schedule was too crammed for pleasure trips into the hills west of town. "That is impossible," she said. "I have other commitments."

To her surprise, he did not brush aside her concern with her other appointments. "That's why I came so early. We can be back by ten. If I'm not mistaken, you had set aside that time for my therapy."

She wrapped her kimono more snugly around her as protection from a trembling that was unrelated to the crisp bite of cool morning air. His recognition of the validity of her schedule reassured her. Unlike other men who had tried to storm the bastions of her defenses, Luke showed a wise acceptance of her livelihood. He did not demand that she cancel her appointments and devote herself solely to his entertainment. His sensitivity touched her more than roses and candlelight.

She concealed her pleasure with a gruff reply. "As long as you're here, you might as well come in and have coffee."

"Wear your boots," he advised. "We're going to be doing some light climbing."

"Watch my lips, Todhunter. I am not going to the mountains."

"You're scared, aren't you? Afraid that after you see the site for the dam you might change your mind."

"I'm not," she protested, leaving the door ajar and traipsing down the hall to the kitchen. "All the trees and flowers and cuddly bunnies that might be drowned aren't going to change the fact that Denver needs water."

"What?" His blue eyes flew wide open in mock surprise. "The lady doesn't care about bunnies? Too bad, Crystal. I had Thumper and Bambi all ready to shake your paw. I promise that we'll be back by ten."

"It's going to be hot and dusty."

"Ten degrees cooler in the mountains. Don't tell me an old native pioneer like yourself is worried about getting messy?"

After a swift debate with her conscience, Crystal acceded to his demands and went upstairs to dress for the mountains. There, where granite cliffs almost touched the sun, their petty problems would find a true perspective.

She wore loose hiking shorts, knee socks and worn leather boots. A faded T-shirt from the Red Zinger Bicycle Race was tucked neatly into her waistband, and she grabbed a red-and-powder-blue jacket in case of rain.

After a quick brushing of teeth and a splash of water on her face, Crystal was ready. The growing excitement of a trip to the mountains filled her with eagerness. She winked at the textbook that lay open on her bedside table. For the next few hours, the therapist would be playing hookey.

She bounded down the stairs and found Luke sitting in one of the wingback chairs in her office with Rorschach on his lap. His talent for placing himself in endearing domestic postures frankly worried her. The temptation to be a Blondie to his Dagwood was getting stronger.

He read to her from the newspaper. "I see where Phoenix is suffering from near drought. Not surprising since we hoard most of the runoff here at the source."

Rorschach mewed his disapproval, and Luke stroked the cat's black-and-white fur. "Don't get all upset, Rory. We'll set things right."

"That cat has no loyalty," she said. "He knows my position on the dam."

"Smart pussy. Recognizes a good opposition when he sees it." Luke looked carefully into Rorschach's eyes. "If I didn't know better, I'd guess that you were a witch and Rory was your familiar. Your eyes are almost identical."

"Thank you very much. I truly adore being compared to a tom."

"You have the same feline quality, and the same enchanting amber flecks in your eyes." Bored by the comparison, Rorschach leaped from Luke's lap and stalked to a sunlit square near the windows. "And you're both standoffish."

"Thanks again." She was aware that he'd laid the newspaper aside and was watching her closely. "Come on into the kitchen. I'll make a thermos of grape juice."

She exited quickly and was surprised when he caught up with her in the kitchen and wrapped his long arms around her waist. "I didn't have a chance last night to thank you. You hustled me out the door so fast I thought you had Robert Redford waiting in your bedroom."

She dug an elbow into his ribs and he released her. "Not everything I do is motivated by lust. Not like some people I could mention."

"That's right. Amber witches are complicated. But I thank you for your magic. I feel like my stutter is gone."

A real happiness surged through her when she turned to face him. "That's wonderful, Luke. Really it is. A winning attitude is half the battle, but I do encourage you to continue with therapy."

"I have every intention of doing so." His smile was warmly compelling. "As long as I can kiss you before I speak, I'll never block again."

She felt as though cold water had been rudely tossed in the face of her silly, approving attitude. "You missed the point, Luke." She pushed him away. "It was the air-flow technique that made it possible for you to speak smoothly."

"I won't believe that." He shrugged and dropped his empty embrace. "It was your kiss. Of course, I don't advocate that particular substitution behavior for any of your other clients."

"That was an accident," she snapped. "And I certainly don't intend to make a regular practice of kiss therapy."

"You shouldn't make promises you can't keep."

"An unusual sentiment for a budding politician." She busied herself making grape juice and locating the thermal jug in a jumbled cabinet to the left of the sink.

"I intend to be an unusual politician. Stalwart and true, above bribes and cigar-smoke confabs. Mr. Clean. Like Jimmy Stewart taking on Washington."

"Interesting comparison. Jimmy Stewart is a stutterer, you know."

"And I'll always take you along to remind me of such pertinent facts." He slapped his thigh. "Are you ready for the mountains, Amber Lady?"

"Stop calling me that." She was insulted by the portrait he'd painted. Her goal was to succeed in her own right, not to become some kind of simpering political appendage, a talisman for the congressman to kiss whenever he needed to make a speech. Unknowingly, he had described one of her worst fears in a few facetious sentences.

From her perspective, the role of politician's consort was even more degrading than being considered a sex object. At least sex objects were desirable. She refused to be a rabbit's foot for him to dangle from his watch chain, smiling and vapid, drawing her identity from his occasional attentions. Her plan to curtail their dawning personal relationship strengthened.

She grabbed a couple of plastic mugs to go with the grape juice and said, "Let's go. I have to be back by ten, and I want to miss rush hour traffic."

"My chariot awaits. A Jeep Wagoneer, vintage 1974. Bumpy, but serviceable."

The traffic was light heading west, but bumper to bumper coming into town. Crystal told him that his first political duty should be the widening of highways and the perfection of mass transit systems.

"I guess so," he said thoughtfully. "Haven't given it much thought. I'm a one-issue candidate."

"There's so much more to be concerned about," she protested. "The schools, new housing developments, taxes, encouraging the arts."

"I know," he said with a resignation unusual for a politician. "After Coyote Creek Dam is defeated, I'm sure I'll hear all about those other things."

"You don't sound too involved with the issues."

"To be completely truthful, I'm not. I haven't taken a stand on anything except the dam."

His apathetic reluctance puzzled her until she had a finger-snapping flash of insight. "I get it. You're using reverse psychology on me."

"What?"

"Sure," she nodded knowingly. "You're being coy, and I'm supposed to tell you how wonderful you could be. I would convince myself that Luke Todhunter is a terrific candidate and end up supporting your position on the dam. Pretty tricky, Todhunter."

He opened his mouth and closed it again. "Maybe you're right."

"Of course, I'm right." She pointed again to the line of cars creeping into downtown Denver. "First you'll have to take care of the transportation problems. Then I might change my mind about the dam."

Crystal subsided into uneasy reflection, deliberately turning her thoughts from the physical presence of the man beside her and launching a brief editorial. She was not one of those short-sighted people who believed the door should be closed on Denver's growth. In her lifetime, she'd seen the city expand from a quiet, unsophisticated burg into a skyscrapered metropolis. She appreciated the heightened cultural level achieved by the newcomers and was proud of her native home, the Queen City of the Plains, a mile high and majestic.

When they turned south off Highway 6 and passed Red Rocks amphitheater, Crystal lost interest in her monologue. Denver—its problems and accomplishments—seemed very far away. An inner peace surged through her. Refreshed by the clean breeze through the open car window, she relaxed in spite of herself. The rugged formations of ruddy sandstone and the sparse, tumbleweed-strewn landscape nurtured her with a complacent sense of well-being.

She glanced at Luke's strong, masculine profile. He seemed to be hewn from this very bedrock, his brow slightly furrowed as he peered into an unfathomable distance. His love for the mountains required no explanation because she shared that feeling. Freedom. Peace. Wonderment. And the feeling that anything was possible.

5

In honor of the mountain scenery, Luke launched into a medley of John Denver tunes in a slightly off-key tenor. His mood fluctuated from pensive to playful. Her comments bothered him and reinforced his doubts about his political skills. He really had no business embarking on a career of statesmanship. The mission had been forced upon him. But the prize was preservation of this natural, awe-inspiring panorama, and for those stakes, he would endure any tactic, no matter how foreign to his nature.

They left the highway and rattled along a narrow road beside a rushing, rippling creek. Loose gravel kicked up by the heavily studded tires of the Jeep clattered a musical counterpoint to his boisterous overture.

"Rocky Mountain h-i-i-igh." He glanced at the slender, amber-eyed lady beside him and was gratified to see her relaxed and contented. Each mile he laid between Crystal and her city responsibilities served to lower her level of tension. The tightness around her mouth smoothed. Her rigid posture eased into a comfortable slouch. She seemed barely cognizant of time and place as her head lolled back against the cracked leather seat.

Her fall of mahogany-colored, wildly curling hair captivated him with its deep richness, and he reached across the distance separating them to give one dangling tendril a sharp yank. "Rocky Mountain high in Colorado," he yodeled the finale.

In his normal baritone voice, he asked, "What do you think? Could I have had a career in music? Was the stage robbed of a bright talent, by a stutter?"

"A lot of singers have speech problems that vanish when they sing." With cheerful sarcasm, she added, "But it's safe to say that you're no Pavarotti."

"Opera? You flatter me." He tried a booming repetition of the word Figaro, only stopping when Crystal clapped her hands over her ears and pleaded.

With a comically self-satisfied grin, he mused, "Wonder if I would stutter in Italian."

"Stuttering is an international disorder," she informed him and continued dryly, "In your case, however, the speech impediment might be an improvement."

"So I've been told." He was not in the least offended. "And how does a nice Denver girl like you come to know so much about opera."

"Really, Luke." She was piqued, but too content to be really angry. "You're not one of those turkeys who think civilization stops at the Mississippi, are you? As a Colorado native, you ought to know better."

She stretched her arms in a feline yawn. The sunlight danced a flickering arabesque across her high cheekbones. "I happen to have been a flower girl at the Central City Opera House."

"No kidding? What color dress did you wear?"

"White, of course." She grinned at the memory. "For purity. Why do you ask?"

"I want to know everything about you. Did you wear long, white gloves?"

"Absolutely. And my dress had these silly little

puffy sleeves. I wasn't daring enough in those days to go strapless. Nor voluptuous enough.'' She briefly surveyed her small-breasted figure and wrinkled her freckléd nose. ''I guess some things never change.''

''Don't put yourself down. I like your body.'' His blue eyes slid from the angle of her shoulders to the firm definition of her calves. He found every inch appetizing, slim and spare, yet utterly feminine. He imagined her as a coltish teen in her white flower-girl dress with a floating swirl of chiffon covering her slender legs, a becoming blush coloring her cheeks.

He compared that vision to the present reality of T-shirt, hiking shorts and scruffy leather boots. She still looked like a teenager, a waifish tomboy who exuded the promise of womanhood. Her mountain-climbing appearance held no hint of the crisp professionalism he had seen in action the night before when she had directed her therapy group with mature competence. Only his unexpected kiss had flustered her.

Luke regretted that moment for the embarrassment it had caused her. His intrusion on her methods was inexcusable, but he had acted on blind instinct, and his subsequent eloquence had somewhat vindicated him. Years of blocking struggling stammers were erased by the magical touch of her lips.

He couldn't help anticipating future kiss therapy as well as more intimate explorations. For the first time, Luke Todhunter was impervious to rejections. He wanted this woman and nothing would change his mind.

She noticed his prolonged scrutiny. ''Mind keeping your eyes on the road, Todhunter?''

''Hold on to your seat. We're heading off the black-top and into the wilderness.''

He expertly guided the Jeep down an unmarked

turnoff just beyond a quaking stand of aspen. Dusty lush vegetation climbed the canyon walls where majestic granite cliffs made a jagged skyline more wonderful than any creation of man. Crystal expelled a long, deep sigh. "I love the mountains."

"More than opera? More than culture?"

"If you're trying to make the point that Denver's civilized population has no right to damage this environment, it is well taken." She raised her index finger like a lecturing pedagogue. "However, the two are not mutually exclusive. I could easily imagine a ballet troupe performing 'Afternoon of a Faun' in this meadow. Culture and nature are compatible. Don't forget the Aspen Music Festival, the chautauquas all over the state, Christo's curtain in Rifle."

"Can't say that I thought much of Christo," he snorted. "Wrapping a canyon in plastic doesn't seem much like art."

"Too avant-garde for you?" she teased. "You're nothing but a stuffy old conservative lawyer."

"Not guilty," he pleaded. "I just didn't have your flower-girl background. Instead of cruising the opera, I was captain of the high-school ski team."

"Am I supposed to be impressed?"

"That was the general idea," he rejoined. "I've skied with Billy Kidd and Jean-Claude Killy."

"Be still my beating heart." She clasped both hands to her breast in a gesture of maidenly thrill. "So have I."

"But have you rock-climbed with James Whittaker?"

"Yep."

"Hiked up Long's Peak?"

"You bet. Twice."

"Owned a season ticket to the Bronco football team in 1967 when Steve Tensi was quarterback?"

"Attended every game with my Uncle Walt."

"How come we never met?" He knew he would never have forgotten an encounter with this Amber Lady. "We must have always been in the same place at different times."

"Disregarding the obvious fact that I was only eight years old when I was attending the Bronco games?"

He groaned in recognition of the nine year age difference that separated them.

"And I was always a little shy," she explained. "I wouldn't have expected the captain of the ski team to give me a second look."

He knew the definition of "a little shy" to a stutterer—it was a diffident attitude that masked fear. panic and sheer terror at being rejected. It was difficult for him to reconcile that image with the cool woman who sat beside him, and he reminded himself to be gentle with her, to show her that he understood the torments.

The groundwork must be carefully constructed since he expected their relationship to last for a lifetime. Slowly, he would build her trust. Patiently, he would fan the sparks until the flame became an all-consuming bonfire.

"What were you like?" she asked. "In with the in crowd? I bet you dated all the cheerleaders."

"I was Mr. Jock," he confirmed. "A real adolescent macho."

Instead of self-effacing bashfulness, Luke had taken the opposite approach to shield himself from close personal relationships. He was an athlete, an acknowledged leader who exuded brashness and false confidence to keep people away. "I was a real tough guy until I went to college back East."

"Then what?"

"A grind. You know the type? The hardworking student who lives in the library."

"Straight A's," she nodded knowingly.

"In law school? Are you kidding? My professors took a dim view of an aspiring trial lawyer who was tongue-tied."

He could see that she was putting the pieces together, and it pleased him. This statement of his fondest ambition would have been threatening if revealed to the wrong person. Another woman might have laughed at the presumption of a stutterer attempting courtroom appearances. Or she might have patted his arm and told him that everything would be all right.

Instead, Crystal displayed an intellectual curiosity. "A trial lawyer," she said, testing the words.

"Contract law was my second choice," he explained. "In spite of your accusation of conservatism, I was a fire-breathing liberal in law school. I wanted to wage every idealistic battle. To be a public defender, to make legality into justice for all."

"I see," she mused. "You wanted to be Superman. Or should I say Superlawyer. With a big, red *L* on your chest."

They exchanged wry grins, not needing to mention that stuttering was his kryptonite. Though he could cite every precedent and thoroughly document each legal point, Luke had never been able to climb atop his soapbox to address a jury. The disappointment still rankled, though now he had reason for hope. Last night, he had successfully addressed a group. Perhaps his dream was not impossible.

If Crystal could cure him, he might pursue his deepest ambition. His feelings for her tangled in a web. He respected her as a therapist and desired her as a woman. With an effort he returned to their conversation. "Maybe I was a little shy, too."

"Don't make me laugh. Whoever heard of a bashful politician."

"Hey, I never wanted to be a candidate," he protested. "All I want is to stop the dam."

"Nobody's twisting your arm," she pointed out.

"This could be the one truly important contribution I make in this life," he said seriously. Perhaps a trace of the liberal still survived in his thinking. Injustice infuriated him, and he sincerely believed that the dam was wrong. "You should realize, Crystal, how hard it is for me to be a spokesperson."

She laid a delicate hand on his hair-roughened forearm. "I know it's tough, Luke. And no matter what else I say or do, no matter how much I disagree with you, I want you to know that I believe in you."

Her encouragement brought him a vital sense of his own power. When she touched him and reassured him, Luke's strength was as unstoppable as an avalanche.

She believed in him! Why did that simple statement seem as if it should be accompanied by the crash of cymbals? What quality of hers caused him to ignite at her simplest gesture?

Crystal withdrew her hand and crossed her legs. He was aroused by the rounded molding of her thigh. A bright aura surrounded her and made him forget everything else. He had never felt so desperately free, nor so determined. A foolish grin crept across his face.

"What, may I ask, is so funny?" Her eyebrows lowered in an expression that he found adorable.

"You. Me. Us. We're funny." He parked the Jeep in a grassy clearing bordered by golden daisies. As the dust settled around them, the boughs of pine wafted their tart pungence. "We're here, my lovely Amber Lady."

"Don't call me Amber," she warned as she alighted from the Jeep. The secluded valley lulled her usually sharp wit. She languorously stretched one leg, then the other before replying, "Funny, eh?"

"That's right. Like a couple of confused rats in a maze who are astonished to find each other."

"You have a mighty strange sense of humor, Todhunter. I didn't even know there was an 'us' to laugh about."

"There will be," he predicted. "Thee and me, Amber Lady. I feel as if I've been waiting for you all my life."

"Did it take you that long to find a woman with dysfluency? It would have been more efficient to put an ad in the classifieds. How about, 'Wanted: Willing babe with stutter for fun and games in the hills.'"

"Nope. It would have been impossible to describe you. I'd have to add intelligent, beautiful, witty, warm, charming, full of amber glow, magical, former flower girl, daughter of geologist, therapist who is able to cure stutterers with a single kiss."

A cloud of worry darkened her features. "Luke, we have to have a serious talk."

"Not now, Amber Lady. Right now, we have to climb."

With long strides, he embarked on a worn path through the pines. When she caught up with him, he was bent over a prickly shrub.

"Luke, I want you to listen to me."

He held out a handful of forage.

"Blueberries," she exclaimed delightedly.

"These are mine. You have to pick your own." He popped a berry into his mouth and proclaimed it delicious. "Hurry up. I promised to get you back by ten."

She hastily plucked the wild berries and chased after him.

Single file, they followed a path worn into a sloping hill of loose, sun-baked gravel. The footing along the trail was easy, rising and falling, but always paralleling a babbling stream that flowed through blueberries, aspen and cottonwood.

They descended to the level of the stream, identified by Luke as the beginning of Coyote Creek and walked side by side through a shaded glen. Climbing again amid boulders, the trail was less clearly marked, evident only to someone who knew the way. They descended to cross the stream, hopping from rock to rock. The cool rush of sparkling water contrasted with sun-warmed surfaces of gray stone.

Crystal knelt on the rocky bank of the stream and scooped up the icy runoff for a drink. The swift current tugged at her fingers. She shrieked with delight when the freezing water touched her mouth. Then, she scooped again. The fresh, clean taste washed through her and dissolved her resolutions. Nothing would be allowed to spoil this moment, this childlike sense of awe. As she watched a twig plummet and eddy over the small rapids, she decided to relax and enjoy this day. Life offered so few peaks to scale, and the well-worn ruts are always waiting.

She bounded to her feet, ran a few steps and spun in a complete, arms-wide-open circle. "This is beautiful, Luke. How much farther?"

His wide smile and sparkling eyes reflected her restored spirits. She couldn't have wished for a better companion.

"Can't you hear it?" he asked. "Right this way."

He pivoted and disappeared between two huge boulders.

Crystal listened. Above the murmur of the stream, she heard a louder rumble. A Steller's jay added his raucous note. The breeze hummed, and a rustling of aspen leaves filled the air. Here was a symphony of nature, so soothing, yet exhilarating.

She squeezed between the massive rocks and entered an enchanted cavern. It wasn't a true cave, but more like a cove hidden among towering pillars of granite. Sun rays pierced the spaces between rocks and lit a waterfall twelve feet high.

Luke sat just inside the shadowed entrance, pitching pebbles into the pooling stream. "Welcome, my Amber Lady, to Merlin's Cave."

She was unable to reply, overcome by the wonder of the place.

"I named it myself," he said with the pride of an explorer. "Found it when I was hiking around back here, picking blueberries. I think this is the most peaceful spot on the earth."

She was touched that he wanted to share his private, secret place with her. "Merlin's Cave," she said. "A good name. It sounds mysterious."

"And challenging. Now we'll see what you're really made of—test your claims of real mountaineering skills." He pointed to the waterfall. "We're going to climb behind the fall. There's another cavern, smaller than this, with a clear pool."

She followed as he clambered over the slippery

rocks. The handholds were wide and safe and not at all difficult. She wondered what other mountaineering test he had in mind.

The second cavern was also illuminated obliquely by cracks in the rocks. As Crystal peered over the edge, she saw Luke unbuttoning his shirt and knew exactly what sort of challenge he had planned. "No way," she said. "This is melted snow. You can take your swim all by yourself."

He shrugged out of the red plaid shirt. "Chicken?"

"Prudent." She hauled herself to the level floor of the second cave and sat cross-legged on a wide, flat rock just beyond the spray of a smaller cascading waterfall. She stuck one finger into the clear pool, snatched it out and shivered. "That's freezing!"

"Not to a real pioneer." He tossed his shirt aside, unbuckled his leather belt and removed it.

Crystal's posture was that of an interested spectator, but when his belt came off, she gulped and hoped he didn't plan on skinny-dipping.

Still wearing his worn Levi's, Luke picked his way around the cave to her side. She noticed the wicked gleam in his eye, and it didn't take a genius to figure out his next move. "Don't you dare," she warned, frantically searching for an escape route. "Don't even think about it."

"What's the matter, my proud beauty?" He came closer. "Afraid of a little water? Where's the old mountain climber spirit?"

"I'm serious, Luke." He caught her forearm in a tight, but playful grasp. "If you throw me in that pool, I'll...."

"Yes?" He whisked her into his arms and off her feet, lifting her as easily as a rag doll. Crystal thrashed

without effect against those muscular arms until their
eyes met and locked, and she ceased her struggle.
"What will you do, my Amber Lady?"

"I'll melt."

Her arms encircled his neck, and she covered his
lopsided grin with a deep kiss. His taste was as fresh
and pure as the glistening waterfall. His powerful
chest felt as strong and enduring as the eternal walls
of stone that surrounded them both.

Luke slid his tongue through her willing lips and
probed the moist cavern within. Her response made
for a passionate duel of thrust and parry that sent
electric thrills coursing through their bodies.

Once freed of her inhibitions, Crystal was relentless. Since Luke's arms were occupied with holding
her, he was helpless to stop her tender flurry of kisses
that ended with a sensuous exploration of his ear. She
traced the intricate shell with her tongue and tickled
the lobe with small nips.

She felt him quiver and heard his breath catch in
his throat as he tried to elude her arousing ministrations. His battle for control only increased her urgent
caresses.

"Stop it, Crystal," he pleaded.

"Chicken?" She breathed into his exquisitely sensitized ear.

He dropped to one knee, balancing his lovely
burden carefully until she rested in a sitting position,
still trapped in his embrace. In the dappled light of his
secret grotto, he raised his hand to her lips and traced
their fullness.

She nuzzled his hand and purred softly as his
fingers followed her jawline and tangled in her hair.
Even her scalp responded to his caress. Her hair was

alive, he. teeth, her fingernails. Every muscle, bone and fiber of her body prickled with longing. She wanted him. No other thought intruded. Their kiss the previous night had orchestrated a sleepless prelude to this wonderful moment of lovemaking.

Crystal dragged her nails across his bared chest, causing a tremor in his taut muscles. His flesh was supple and warm in the cool, dark recesses of Merlin's Cave. Vibrant life flowed between them.

Luke's hand searched beneath her T-shirt, cupping her small breast and tantalizing the peak to hard readiness. As he tugged the thin material higher, she pulled it in the opposite direction.

"Don't," he murmured. "I want to see you."

"There's not much to see." She lowered her eyes, self-conscious about the size of her breasts as he removed her shirt.

"What's there is choice," he rejoined. "Your body is perfect, exactly the way a woman should be." His hand rested on her shoulder and slid to her upper arm. "Here you're strong. These are firm, capable arms." His lips descended to her trembling biceps, then glided at a right angle to tease the hardened nipple of her swelling breast. "But you're soft here. Pliant and giving."

His kisses followed the smooth line of her throat to her lips, and he gathered her to him. The meeting of their bodies satisfied and stimulated her. Her eyelids felt heavy, but she was totally awake, aroused to sensations she had never before experienced.

He gave voice to her emotions. "God, Crystal, this is so good." His rumbling baritone blended with the constant thrum of the waterfall in a natural harmony. It *was* good. The warmth of their flesh in the misted cavern was as natural as the earth and water surrounding them.

He began to lower her gently to the smooth, cold rock, but she instinctively recoiled from its frigid hardness.

"My shirt," he said. "It's way over there."

She propped herself in a sitting posture. "I can wait."

He reached quickly and spread the crimson plaid behind her for a thin cushion. "Will you be comfortable?"

"I'll live," she said huskily. She pulled him to her as she reclined. Though she tried to convince him that the rough stone was sweet as a down pillow, she couldn't help but gasp when her back made contact with the moist, hard surface. The sloping rock was not made for human contours, and her head rested lower than the rest of her body with her unbound hair nearly dangling in the icy pool.

Grinning down at her, Luke said, "I never promised you a rose garden, but this is ridiculous." He clambered to a kneeling posture and scooped her into his arms. "Let's move over to that spot."

"I'm not helpless." She protested as much against the forces that were thwarting their lovemaking as at his plan to seek a more comfortable rock. "I can walk."

"Don't fight me now, Crystal." He struggled, off balance with her weight. His leather-soled boots slipped. With a surprised yell, he staggered backward and carried her along with him.

The ice-cold waters of the pool quickly doused her desire. She shuddered convulsively when her head broke the surface of the chest-deep pond. "Nice work,

Todhunter," she sputtered. "You sure know how to sweep a lady off her feet."

His laughter echoed through the cavern. "Nothing like a cold shower."

She heaved her body onto the rock beside the pool, aware of the shocked tingling from the freezing liquid.

"Where are you going?" he yelled. "Come under the waterfall with me. You're already wet."

"I've had enough." She was angry with herself. How easily she'd succumbed to his spell! Merlin's Cave, this private grotto of enchantment where the world vanished, was too like a cool, dark Eden.

"You said you'd have me back by ten," she accused. "That leaves less than an hour for the drive." She raised her fist in a threatening gesture. "That is if my watch still works—which I suppose it doesn't."

He dove under the water and resurfaced at her feet. His blond hair was dark and sleek as a seal. As he pulled himself out, she was hypnotized anew by his splendid physique. He shook himself like a wet puppy and diamond drops of water fell from him. More than a mortal man, he was a perfect Apollo, a sun god.

Swiftly, she looked away. She willed her mind to blankness as she began to retrace her route down into the lower cavern.

"Crystal, wait. There's a better way."

She narrowed her eyes suspiciously. "If this is another one of your tricks, I'll strangle you."

He grabbed both her arms in his huge hands and forced her to confront him. "Listen, lady. There's something you're going to learn about me."

"L-l-let go of m-m-my arms." The flip-flop palpitations of her heart released her stutter. She stood before him, wet and woebegone. How could she reject him? She wanted him so badly that she could again feel the urgent throb of her desire.

"You'd better know that I'm a man of my word. When I make a promise, I mean it. Since it's so important to you, we will be back at ten."

"Am I supposed to be g-g-grateful?"

He sighed. His voice softened. "I promise you, Crystal Baxter, that someday we will be one. One heart. One breath. One life. You won't escape me."

He placed a single, gentle kiss on her forehead to seal his vow. Then, his grip loosened. He picked up his shirt and beckoned her to follow.

She scrambled after him pulling on her T-shirt. With each step she could have kicked herself. What a mess she'd made of this whole ordeal. Instead of calmly stating her good intentions, she had surrendered to the magic of his mysterious caves. What would have happened if they hadn't collapsed into the freezing pool?

Crystal knew. She wasn't a tease. If she had allowed it, the certain outcome would have been a glorious, wonderful consummation of their passion. Her mind skimmed over that possibility, fearful of the trembling promise. Fortunately, lovemaking on the rocks had proven logistically impossible.

She accidentally jammed her toe against a jagged edge. "Idiot," she said aloud.

"What?"

"I was talking to myself." She hoped he hadn't heard.

"Idiot?" He dashed her hope. "You can't seriously say that to Crystal Jane Baxter, almost-a-Ph.D."

Luke stretched out his hand and pulled her onto a

wide pinnacle of rock, into harsh, sunlit reality. "It's all downhill from here," he said. "You want my shirt? It's dry."

"Just give me a few minutes in the sun." She flopped onto the hard granite and propped her chin on her fists, shivering as a mountain breeze touched her damp, clinging T-shirt. Snowcapped peaks shone in the distance. Overhead, a lonely hawk circled slowly and dove into the treetops. This was the right place to tell him. Open and free on top of the world, she could scream her fool head off and not another soul would hear.

"Luke, I have something to say to you. And I want you to sit quietly and listen."

He spread his long legs straight before him to dry in the sun. "You only have five minutes if we're going to stay on schedule. Shoot."

She fired from the hip. "I can't be your therapist. I've already compromised myself in front of my therapy group, and the situation can only get worse. As I mentioned last night, I will refer you to someone else."

"Does this colleague also practice kiss therapy?"

"Don't interrupt." She had built a full head of steam and wanted to get this over with. "Also, I am at the brink of finishing my dissertation for my doctorate. I don't need to tell you—a graduate of law school—how demanding academic studies can be. I have no time whatsoever for a personal life."

"Are you finished?"

"Not quite." She drew a ragged breath that left a queasy emptiness in the pit of her stomach. "I can't see you anymore. At least not for a month or two. Not until I've finished my course work."

She stared past him at the serrated spires of ponderosa pine. There. She'd told him. It was over. Instead of release, she felt her arms prickling with wet cold, the soft hairs rising. Then heat, and the churning knot in her stomach twisted again. The landscape blurred before her as she blinked away her unshed tears.

"Sorry, Crystal. I won't accept that."

"You have no choice, Luke." Despite her stated rejection, her heart beat faster and her spirit ascended like the hawk soaring above the valley. "This is not open for negotiation."

"As far as personal involvement goes, I can understand. You have set a difficult course, and I would never stand in your way. Even though I can't see how my caring would interfere, that's your decision. If you want to go through this last academic phase alone, I can respect that."

"Thank you."

"Even though I would humbly prepare your dinner every evening and file your note cards and carry your books, I acknowledge your stubborn need to be totally self-sufficient."

Crystal's chin thrust forward. She should have been angered by his teasing, but his humor was so gentle she could hardly keep from smiling.

"Even though I would devote myself to saving you time and energy," he continued. "Even though I would guarantee you a physical release to relax and energize you, I can concede the point. Even though . . . ."

"Hold it right there. I refuse to be seduced by the fantasies of a self-confessed macho." She remembered the aftermath of last night's embrace—sleeplessness and an inability to work. Relationships demanded time, and that was presently in short supply. "I'm not going to change my mind."

"Fair enough. I can wait for your affection, but I can't postpone my therapy. I came to you because you're the best, and you proved that. Last night was the first time in my life I was able to speak before a group without stuttering."

She almost told him that it was a fluke, but the therapist in her cautioned against damaging his newly gained self-esteem. "You accomplished that speech all by yourself, Luke. Another therapist can build and continue on your success."

"I don't want another therapist. I want you. I trust you and believe in you. I've spent all my life balancing on a tightrope, afraid to go forward and afraid to go back. You've given me a reason to move and a balancing pole for stability. Don't take that away from me, Crystal."

"But how can I treat you? I can't be kissing you every time you have to speak."

"I'll do anything you say. You name the methods."

Crystal rested her cheek on her hands and studied his face. Though his features were arranged in serious contemplation, his eyes mirrored a devilish challenge. She couldn't in good conscience refuse to help him, not when they already had made such significant progress. His request was reasonable and logical. If she refused to treat him, she would be turning her back on the very reason she had chosen her profession. Yet, how could she hope to spend time in his company without transgressing the boundaries of professional decorum? "I'm damned if I do, and damned if I don't," she said.

"Some people are just lucky," he sympathized. "Try to think of it as being stuck between a rock and a hard place."

The farewell scene she had visualized was far different from the reality. She had expected high drama and instead was finding herself cast in a musical comedy. Luke's repartee was as seductive as his warm embrace.

A quicksilver thought flashed through her mind. Loving Luke could be fun. He made her laugh and vanquished the stress that tainted much of her scheduled life. Only once—when he had promised her that they would be one—had the intensity of his nature intruded.

As her eyes traveled over the chiseled planes of his face, she saw a challenge. His lifted eyebrow and the slight curl of his lip dared her to share his amusement, like the game played by children to see who can keep from laughing first.

Against her better judgment, Crystal decided to partake of this private joke. If his therapy took too much of her time, she could always call a halt. Or could she?

With a stern expression, she outlined her conditions. "I will work with you. However, you must agree to the following." She listed them on her fingers. "No more kiss therapy. You will be on time. You will complete all assignments. You will depart on schedule."

"I do solemnly promise." His blue eyes twinkled in acceptance of his victory. "My lovely Amber Lady."

"And you will not call me that name," she said strictly. "I mean it, Luke. One slip and the deal is off. You'll have to find yourself another therapist. I am henceforth to be known as Crystal. Hard and cold and distant."

He nodded obediently. "So what's my next assignment?"

"*Goldilocks and the Three Bears*. Tomorrow at one o'clock you will be the afternoon storyteller at the Children's Museum."

6

CRYSTAL ALWAYS ENJOYED the free-wheeling, creative atmosphere of the Children's Museum. Her spirits lifted when she passed through the flowing, colorful mural at the front entrance and picked her way through papier-maché dragons, orange-silk parachute canopies and a swarm of waist-high munchkins wearing Indian war paint.

After the daily grind of dry textbooks and adult problems, the purposeful nonsense of the educational exhibits—including anatomical diagrams of superheros, a wardrobe trunk full of clothes from other lands, a skeleton named Fred and an incubator for baby chicks—always refreshed and renewed her.

She greeted the woman at the front desk who was wearing insect antennae and huge sunglasses and told her to expect a tall, blond man in a business suit who would assist during today's session of storytelling and diagnosing speech problems.

She had arranged with the museum staff to volunteer on a weekly basis as the resident storyteller. With her picture books and unfinished sentences, she tested small groups in the guise of resident storyteller. The children with obvious disorders, like stuttering and lisps, were easily spotted, but the more complex disorders required her alert expertise. Crystal approached each session with enthusiasm and left feeling as though she had accomplished something important.

"Today might be the exception," she said to herself as she finished arranging her test materials and checked her wristwatch. It was ten minutes to one o'clock. Luke wasn't late yet, but he was certainly cutting it close. On their way back into town yesterday, she had been very sure that he understood his assignment. He could only benefit from group speaking situations, and she figured that a group of children would provide a nonthreatening arena for him to test his wings.

Crystal paced the short length of the room and felt the seconds slip by like sand in an hourglass. Where was he? The placard outside the Special Events room announced one o'clock as the time for the storyteller. Smaller print advised parents to register at the front desk where the speech pathology tests were explained on a neatly printed card and permission slips were signed.

She couldn't wait any longer. Slowly, she opened the door. "Hello," she greeted a sturdy, tow-headed four-year-old.

"Hi. My name is Jason." He stomped into the room and started making faces at himself in the mirror. Soon, other children wandered in, intent on choosing the best seats—close to the storyteller.

As she collected permission slips from the museum attendant, she asked if a tall, blond man had arrived.

"Not that I know of."

"If he comes within the next ten minutes, please show him into the Special Events room."

How could he be late? All his sincere promises and commitments were negated by his tardiness. Crystal fumed silently and dragged her attention back to the children.

"All right, kids. Gather around." Crystal took her place on a low stool, wanting to be as close to the children as possible. "Jason, you come sit by me."

"That's a pretty thing you have on."

"Is it on my arm?" She displayed the bright pink bracelet that matched her neck scarf and the stripe in her short-sleeved jacket. Her clothing was selected with an eye to vivid colors and patterns for her sessions with the children.

"Nope," said Jason, shaking his white-blond head. "It's up here."

"On my neck?

"Yeah. It's a scarf.

"Thank you, Jason. That was a lovely compliment. Would you repeat it, please?"

"Yeah." He glowed with his accomplishment. "That's a pretty scarf."

Crystal cheerfully greeted the five other children and asked them to introduce themselves and tell their ages. She listened carefully to their enunciation, trying to overcome her anger at the absent Luke. All the children were fairly fluent except for a skinny wide-eyed black boy. "I d-d-don't g-got to say nothing."

Crystal judged his age to be about five, probably in kindergarten. "May I guess your name?"

He pulled the corners of his mouth into a frown, but nodded curtly.

"Is it Peter or Harry or John? William? Franklin or George?" She glanced at the note cards in her lap which the parents had filled out, and read his name. "Everett Jackson?"

His eyes narrowed, but the frown was less pronounced.

"How old are you, Everett?"

"F-f-f-f-" He gave up the effort and held up an open hand.

"I'm pleased to meet you, Mr. Jackson. Now I'll tell you my name. Crystal Baxter. Since we are all friends, you may call me Crystal. I am a speech therapist. Does anyone know what that means?" She purposely looked beyond the waving hands and stared at Everett.

He responded. "Y-y-yeah. You a sh-sh-shrink." The disgust in his utterance was obvious, and Crystal understood why his mother had written on the note card under comments, "He stutters. Help."

If Crystal had taken the time to review the note cards before the children gathered around her, she might have avoided this situation. Everett's acute condition was not appropriate for a diagnostic session. There was no question that he needed further therapy. Crystal blamed Luke. His absence had disrupted her usual efficiency.

"Everett is right," she said. "Some of the methods I use were developed by psychologists. Mostly I use words, all the words in the whole world. I think my favorite is peanut butter. Jason, what's your favorite word?"

"Llama. I went to the zoo."

"I like elephants," piped a tiny girl.

"Thank you for telling us, Lynn.... All right, children. I'm going to ask you several questions while I'm telling you a story. You will only answer when I say your name. Is that understood?" Her voice was firm. She'd learned to keep these sessions moving quickly, well within their limited attention spans.

She read off each name on the cards and wrote it on a stick-on tag. As she gave the tags to the children, she made eye contact and asked them for their favorite word. When she got to Everett, he answered quickly.

"G-g-g-gun."

She groaned silently. A junior psychopath. Was he trying to shock her? She reached out, grasped his arm and applied the name tag to his skinny chest. Further argument was stifled by the entrance of another person into the room. Crystal followed the path of the children's eyes, swiveled on her stool and saw Luke, casually handsome in a pale-blue, pin-striped seersucker suit.

She wrote "Mr. Luke" on a name tag and explained his presence. "Mr. Luke is also a storyteller. After we finish some of our exercises, he will talk to you. Would you please sit on the floor with the children, Mr. Luke?"

She took perverse pleasure in seeing the dignified lawyer-congressional candidate sprawled on the orange shag carpet and hoped the discomfort would begin to repay him for being late.

She launched into her first story, an eerie ghost tale that had been lavishly illustrated by an artist friend. For one-to-one work, a tamer story was possible, but Crystal used more extreme methods to hold the attention of the preschoolers. The purpose of her fill-in-the-blanks story was to discover certain patterns in the substitution of inappropriate word choices.

"The head of the monster was as high as the roof. He wasn't short. He was very.... Everett, can you give me a word?"

"B-b-bad." His expression told her that he had deliberately substituted the wrong word.

She continued. "He ate up all the spinach in town.

He ate up all the peas. He never ever said thank you. He never said.... What's the word, Melissa?''

"Please."

She finished the story. Two of the children had revealed unusual responses. "Okay, children. Let's go to the mirror."

A long mirror decorated one wall. It was here that Crystal noted unusual formations of sounds and possible physical defects. "I want you all to make a face like the green monster. Okay, freeze. Nobody move."

The tall, blond figure loomed over the children, his arms spread and fingers extended like talons. The gargoyle expression on his face made Crystal laugh aloud. "That is one bad monster. Don't you think so, Everett?"

The boy turned wide, hostile eyes up a Luke Todhunter, and the big man snarled. Everett grinned and snarled back.

As Crystal went through the mouth and tongue exercises, Luke followed her instructions to the letter. The children thoroughly enjoyed his mouthing, and the hour progressed more smoothly than she had expected.

"All right, kids. Back to the story-telling stool. Mr. Luke is going to tell you a story."

Their response was enthusiastic. Melissa clung to Luke's arm and seated herself right beside the long-legged playmate.

"Whenever you are ready, Mr. Luke. Please begin."

"Once upon a t-t-time." Luke took a deep breath and started over. "Once upon a t-t-t-time. There w-w-w-was a p-p-princess."

Everett leaped to his feet. "He m-m-making f-fun."

"No," Luke protested with anguish in his eyes.

A redheaded girl looked to Crystal. "What's the matter with him? Can't he talk?"

"It's a joke," said Jason confidently.

"Ain't f-f-funny," Everett shouted, near to tears.

Crystal was shocked. She had never expected Luke to have such difficulty in this situation. From the pained expression on his face, she guessed that he was reliving horrible memories from his own childhood.

Jason began a singsong chant. "M-m-mr. L-l-l-luke. See, it's funny. Like the m-m-monster."

Crystal rose up on her knees and clapped her hands once for attention. "Sit down, Everett. Now you will all see what a speech therapist does. Mr. Luke is not teasing anyone. Nor is he trying to be funny. Mr. Luke is a stutterer."

Everett sank to a heap on the floor. "L-like m-m-me? B-b-but he all growed up."

"Many grown-ups stutter. Now, I'm going to show you how Mr. Luke can overcome his problem." She stepped to Luke's side. Her palms were sweating, and she felt a quavering at the base of her own throat. Her insensitive approach to Luke's speech impediment may have set him back terribly. If he couldn't handle a group of unruly children, how could he ever succeed at a town meeting with sophisticated, hostile adults. She read that fear in his eyes as she laid her hands on his shoulders. "Take a deep breath. And, children, you take a deep breath. Take another."

The atmosphere in the cheery room was electric. "Roll your head around on your neck. Just like we were doing at the mirror."

She concentrated on Luke. "Now I want you all to speak while you breathe. Say, hello, Sunshine."

His deep baritone rumbled over the frail voices of

the children. Crystal exhaled with pure relief. He wasn't stuttering. "Say, hello, Rain. Take another breath. Hello, Flowers. Another breath. Come again."

She stared into Luke's cobalt eyes as he repeated the exercise. She saw confusion. His lips formed nonsense words, but his expression showed concern. She spoke softly to him. "Are you ready?"

He shook his head, and she imagined a confused little boy trying to put words together, words that stuck in his throat. She sympathized with the child who still lived within the man, but she offered him no pity. She knew he had wellsprings of strength to draw upon. Only his willpower would overcome the stutter.

"Okay, kids. Let's go the the chalkboard."

An exercise to encourage the rhythmic flow of speech was to draw loops along the board. She got the children started, then pulled Everett aside. "I want you to help me. Mr. Luke stutters just like you do. I want you to work together."

She seated the two males together in a corner and told Luke to teach the air-flow technique to Everett. The big blond head and the small black one bent together, sharing a common bond. Soon, they were giggling like cohorts plotting a practical joke to spring on Crystal. Luke signaled that he was ready to begin again.

Again, the children gathered around. Crystal's heart thumped so hard in her breast that she feared her nervousness was audible.

"Once upon a time," Luke started smoothly. His use of the air-flow technique was barely apparent. "There was a boy who couldn't run. He huffed and puffed."

Luke looked at Everett, and the little boy provided sound effects of loud panting.

"But he just couldn't run. All the other children ran like the wind."

Everett circled the room at a speedy gallop.

"But this little boy couldn't get his feet to go any faster than this."

Everett provided the sound and the action: "Plop. Plop. Plop."

"The boy went to the barnyard to talk with the horses."

Everett whinnied.

The story went all through the barnyard with appropriate sound effects for each animal.

"And one fine day, when the boy was down by the pond, he started talking to a big green frog. This was a beautiful frog with black spots and huge yellow eyes as big as saucers. And this frog said she was a princess of frogs."

"B-b-but can she run?" Everett asked.

"She told him that frogs don't run. They jump from lily pad to lily pad, and the noise they make is something like this...."

"Plop. Plop. Plop."

"So, the boy held the frog in his hand. Put his nose right up against hers and said, 'I'm a boy, not a frog. I need to run.' Well, this frog princess kissed that boy, right on the nose."

Everett made a huge smacking sound.

"And she told him to go ahead and run, not to think about it, just to put his feet on the ground and run. Do you know what happened?"

The children chorused their encouragement.

"That boy let his feet do his talking. And his feet went fast."

Everett started running.

"Fast. Can you show me how to run really fast?"

Before Crystal could object, the whole group of children were on their feet, dashing around the small room like a stream of supercharged molecules. Luke shouted, "Stop."

He looked down on the giggling faces surrounding him. "Do you believe in frog princesses?"

"Yeah!"

Then his eyes rose above the children's heads and focused on the amber reflections in Crystal's. "Sometimes, you'll find a princess right in your own backyard. Someone who has been there all along, but you never noticed. And when you do, never let her go because she's magic."

"And she m-m-makes you r-run good," Everett added knowingly.

Crystal felt an unreasoning pride blossoming within her. She could barely contain the explosion of happiness. She lowered her eyelids and clenched her jaw to keep from bursting.

The children demanded another fable, but Crystal stopped their cries. "Sorry, kids. That's all for today. Let's quickly do the vocabulary book, and then it's time to go."

Luke turned the pages while Crystal questioned the children. Their cooperation carried over into this exercise, and she was able to make notes on the cards which would be returned to their parents. On Everett's card, she wrote, "See me." She recommended further tests for one child and remarked to the parent of a girl with an excellent vocabulary that her daughter might be gifted. Despite her earlier confusion and hostility, Crystal had found this session particularly productive. Her good cheer was evident as she bid the children farewell and closed the door behind them.

"So, Mr. Luke, you think I'm a frog?"

"The most beautiful frog in the pond."

"I have a good mind to give you a couple of warts." She went to him and touched his nose. "Starting here."

He closed his eyes and puckered his lips. "I'm ready."

"Yuck," she teased, backing away from him and ending with arms akimbo and head cocked to one side, regarding his foolishness with fond indulgence. She guessed that the damage to his ego had been repaired. Only a truly confident person would act like such a fool.

To him she said, "Do you know what my father would call you?"

"Probably one of those rock names. Bullion? Molybdenum?"

"Dear old dad would say you were an *R*. Ready as rain. Randy as a rooster. Rabid as a rattlesnake."

"Does your father use a lot of these charming down-home homilies?"

"He can be a veritable backwoods philosopher when he wants to be." Crystal began tidying up the room. With sweeping strokes, she cleaned the blackboard. "It was often like being raised by Pappy Yokum."

"Was your mother like Mammy, feisty, with a corn-cob pipe?" He stacked her books and materials and placed them neatly on the stool.

"Surely you jest. Mama was gentility personified. I can't imagine how she's handling life in the Yukon." She paused thoughtfully. "Maybe she loves it. I never really understood her. She seemed so preoccupied with cooking and cleaning for us four kids, but one night when I couldn't sleep, I caught her. She was reading Virginia Woolf and she looked up at me and said, 'Do you consider yourself a feminist, dear?'"

"I bet you nodded your tiny head."

"I was only eleven or twelve. I didn't know what to say. So, she patted my head, told me to think about it and got a cold glass of milk from the refrigerator. What about you? What kind of relationship did you have with your family?"

Luke picked up the book about the green monster. "The illustrations for this book are fantastic. Where did you find it?"

Crystal recognized the ploy—he had changed the subject too quickly. There must be something significant about his family relationships. She made a mental note to probe when they had some time.

She took the book from his hand. "This is an original. The pictures were done by a friend who is an artist." She lowered her eyebrows. "And don't even ask to meet her. She's tall and lithe and has magnificent blond hair down to her waist. The lady is altogether too much of a threat."

"Do I detect a note of jealousy?" His self-satisfied smirk spoke volumes. "I hope you're finally realizing what a catch I am."

"Jealous of your affections? You're a monster, Todhunter. Fully as beastly as the pictures in this book." She waved the note cards. "See if you can find something to amuse yourself. I have to chat with a couple of parents."

"May I call my office, boss lady?"

"Sure. If you're not too busy, you can even walk me home."

"Walk?" he questioned.

"Surely you remember walking, Ferrari man? One foot in front of the other? It's not far and lots easier than finding parking places this close to downtown."

"The sacrifices I make for you." He gallantly held the door. "I'll meet you out front by the talking dragon."

7

CRYSTAL WATCHED WITH AMUSEMENT as three of the children from her testing session pounced on Mr. Luke. He was dragged, feebly protesting, to share the wonderful exhibits in the Children's Museum.

She quickly reassured and dismissed the waiting parents, except for Everett's mother. Since Everett was safely attached to Luke, Crystal was able to grasp a moment of privacy with the slender, elegant black woman whose concern for her son was evident.

There were no surprises in the mother's revelations that Everett was bright, hostile and a behavior problem in kindergarten. Crystal had seen enough children to recognize Everett as a kid who could eat therapists for lunch. Reluctantly, she agreed to take over his treatment, hoping she could build on the trust she had established in this first meeting.

Throughout her serious discussion with Everett's mother, Crystal kept thinking of Luke the gargoyle, and it was only with extra willpower that Crystal maintained her professional decorum.

Her bubbly mood persisted as she hurried through the mundane filing and reporting duties required of museum volunteers and finally went in search of her lighthearted nemesis.

She found Luke Todhunter, candidate for high political office, completely fascinated with a water recycling exhibit. Several hollow, galvanized pipes were interconnected with plastic tubes to make a visual sluice. Water flowed into a huge, iron vat and was recirculated by a pump. Luke followed the course of a Ping-Pong ball inside a tube with intense concentration. His small companions showed more excitement about dipping into the water and shaking wet balls at each other.

He glanced up and saw her. "Take a look at this, Crystal." He flipped her a Ping-Pong ball. "See how efficiently water can be used and reused."

She immediately caught the hint. "Why, yes, Luke. If we could get the city of Denver to build this exhibit on a grand scale, there would be no need for dams. Only two million Ping-Pong balls for the populace."

"Makes a great campaign slogan: A Pong in every pot."

"As soon as you can tear yourself away, I do have another appointment."

"Always rushing." He drew his hands from the water, revealing soggy cuffs. Splashing droplets decorated the pale blue of his suit. The situation was the very opposite of the wallpaper debacle when she had been a mess and he was cool and neat. Perhaps his comment at that time applied just as well to this moment. He was involved.

As they strolled past the other exhibits, Luke commented on the excitement and creativity of the Children's Museum. "How come I've never been here before?"

"You just don't know the right people."

They stopped beside the talking dragon for Luke to make a phone call. Crystal deposited her testing materials at the front desk and returned to find him engaged in angry conversation.

"It will wait," he snapped, "because I say it will wait. Let me speak with Ms Baumann."

His jaw was set in firm determination, his blue eyes wintry cold. This was a Luke Todhunter that Crystal had never seen—a hard-driving attorney who practiced contract law. "In my lower right hand drawer, Ms Baumann, you will find the lien on our client's property. When Westfall arrives, have him sign the release. You can notarize his signature."

As he held the telephone and listened, Crystal wondered why she had never noticed the hard lines around his mouth. Despite his nervous finger-tapping on the receiver, his voice remained cool and masterful. "It's a standard procedure, Ms Baumann. Merely an exchange of collateral for lease-hold improvements. You can handle Westfall. He's no match for the best legal secretary in town."

Crystal imagined a cooing Ms Baumann at the other end of the line as he gave further instructions carefully buffered by judicious praise. His talent for manipulation cast a shadow over her bright and happy mood. She saw how very easily he obtained his goals. Was she just another challenge for him? Before he hung up, she overheard him say that he wouldn't be in for the rest of the day.

So that's his game, she said to herself. *Spend the rest of the day—and the night?—with me.* In spite of all those promises that she could call the shots, Luke was plotting. She made a mental vow to stand firm in her resolutions. Their relationship would be strictly therapeutic. No kissing. No embracing. No future entanglements.

With a calm, noncommittal expression, she joined him. "Ready for our walk?"

"What's the matter?" In an instant, he had pierced her staid pose. "You look like Crystal, not Amber."

"That's because I am Crystal. Let's go."

Heat from the relentless August sun struck them as soon as their feet touched the white concrete pavement. The museum had been air-conditioned and when the door closed on the happy shouts of children, it was like walking into a harsh environment where the roar of traffic assaulted them and the wind was dead.

"You really want to walk?" he said, loosening his tie. "The Ferrari is air-conditioned."

"I went with you to the mountains so you could show me the beauty of Coyote Creek," she reminded. "I'll return the favor by reintroducing you to Denver."

She strode determinedly past the low-slung sports car. Beneath the windshield wiper, a yellow parking ticket adorned the window. "Not an auspicious beginning for an aspiring congressman," she commented.

"It's your fault, you know. I was in such a hurry to get to your assignment on time that I forgot the parking meter."

"And you were still late. That says something about the quality of your promises."

"I was right on time," he protested. "I walked into that room on the stroke of one."

"Really, Luke—" she pulled a disapproving face "—I am capable of telling time."

He grabbed her forearm and held their watches side by side. His was five minutes slower, but Crystal was

unaware of the difference. The simple touch of his
hand had awakened in her a tremulous thrill she had
sworn to prohibit. When his arm rubbed against hers,
she imagined she could feel the rough, blond hairs of
his arm through his shirt-sleeve and his damp jacket.
Her pulse quickened to a tango beat. The heat was
overwhelming.

"See," he said. "Your watch must have been dam-
aged in the mountains yesterday. You're fast."

"I beg your pardon."

His momentary confusion at her response dissolved
in a chuckle. "Your watch is fast. Your morality, however is synchronized at a pace set in the Victorian
era."

"Why should we assume that *my* watch is wrong?"
she demanded with a rage out of proportion with the
simple misunderstanding. "I'd say that you're slow."

"I'm set with the clock on the Civic Center."

"That is a decoration, all Roman numerals and
bonging bells. It is almost never accurate."

They crossed the street and came in sight of that
cupola tower. Columns and porticos stretched majes-
tically across a wide-staired, marble facade. The clock
agreed with Luke, but he conceded that accuracy was
not one of its best features.

In the grassy park opposite the Capitol Building,
they dodged a Frisbee. Crystal set a rapid pace, her
mind racing as she struggled to control the emotion
raised by his nearness.

"Slow down, frog princess. This is one boy who
doesn't need to be taught to run." He faked utter ex-
haustion, leaning his arm on her shoulder. Crystal
shrugged him off in annoyance. Why did he have to
keep touching her?

"I'm going to be treating Everett," she announced. "I talked with his mother."

"I'm glad, but jealous. The kid could be a charmer if he put his mind to it."

"Don't worry about that. According to his mother, he's already been through three therapists."

"Are we talking about Everett? My sound-effects man?" He shook his head in disbelief. "Must have been the wrong therapists. That kid is dynamite. I could understand if you told me that snotty, little Jason was a therapy problem."

"Why?"

"Didn't you hear? L-l-luke is f-f-funny." He bit his lower lip, and Crystal found it hard to reconcile his hurt little-boy expression with his usual confidence.

"I'm sorry about that, but he's only a child. I'm sure he didn't mean to upset you."

"Oh yes, he did. I've heard all the arguments about the unconscious cruelty of children, and they don't make a damn bit of sense. Age is no excuse. Your little Jason is a tow-headed rat who almost had his skinny neck wrung."

"I guess I can scratch 'love of children' from your list of sterling qualities," she said wryly. Though his tone was even, she recognized an underlying vulnerability.

"When Jason started that chant, I went right back to kindergarten in my mind." He shook his head to dispel the painful memories.

"It might interest you to know that Jason also has a language problem. He really could benefit from regular therapy, but his mother is reluctant to take that step."

"She'd rather use your free group, eh?" His knowing nod reminded her that attorneys were also called upon frequently for free advice.

They hurried across the street on a yellow caution light. Crystal had to scamper to match Luke's long-legged strides.

"How early do you start therapy?" Luke asked suddenly.

"As soon as a problem is recognized. Early correct patterning can save hours of reconditioning. In some obvious cases—like hearing loss and cleft palate—we start them as young as two years."

"Before they're out of diapers," he said with surprise. "What about stutterers?"

"That's more difficult to diagnose. Many children stutter when they're first learning to speak. It's like riding a bicycle. You have to fall off a few times before you get it right. Generally speaking, I would not treat language dysfluency in toddlers unless there was an apparent physical cause."

They sidestepped a group of tourists and mounted the stairs to the Capitol Building. The shining gold dome proclaimed Colorado's wealth, its mines of gold and silver and years of frontier tradition. As usual, the clarion voice of a tourist guessed at the probable value of the gold-plated dome. Crystal squinted into its bright reflection and said under her breath, "I've always thought it was a bit ostentatious."

"I like it," Luke announced. "A proud structure for a proud state."

"Spoken like a politician. Just think, after the election, you'll be climbing these steps with important matters of state in your attaché case."

"Not necessarily. Remember—the thrill of victory and the agony of defeat."

He paused at the top of the stairs and rested one rough hand on the lead cannon monument. His eyes assumed a faraway look, and Crystal could see his frontiersman heritage in the chiseled lines of his face. His face intrigued her—capable of being hard and humorous and somehow noble.

"You were right," he said. "It's been too long since I walked through Denver. Remember when no building could be taller than this gold dome? Now downtown is twenty stories high, all new and shiny."

Crystal followed his gaze. "It takes a native to appreciate how much Denver has changed."

"Do you remember the elm before the blight? The free musicals in Cheesman Park? The narrow-gauge railroad?"

Each of his comments struck a common chord in her memory. The nuances of her past harmonized so well with his. Denver. The mountains. The west. He was playing their song.

She almost laid her hand atop his, but recalled that she was supposed to be wary. His instruction to his secretary—that he would be out of the office for the rest of the day—betrayed his motivations. Perhaps he meant to seduce her with sweet nostalgia.

"I like the changes," she asserted. "There's the Art Museum." She pointed to the magnificent castle at the south end of the park. "And the Sixteenth Street Mall. And Larimer Square. I'm pleased with the way my city has grown up."

In light of his rabid environmentalist stand, his agreement surprised her. "When I was younger, I thought Denver had everything I wanted, but every change seems to fulfill me even more. The mountains are my deep and abiding solace, but Denver is like a charming mistress—just when I think I've tired of her diversions, she shows me another side."

Crystal pointed out the obvious argument in favor of Denver's continued growth. "Which is precisely why Coyote Creek Dam is a necessity. We need the water."

He turned his head toward the gold-plated Capitol dome, the sun on his hair creating its own golden highlights. "There are other technological methods of improving our water supply. No need for Denver to rape the environment that has served her so well."

"Aren't your alternatives awfully expensive?"

"All change is expensive." His blue-eyed gaze fell to her face, and she knew that their generalized conversation was subtly turning specific. "You have to give up something to take the next step forward."

What did he expect her to give up? Her academic accomplishments? Her therapy practice? "I don't know what you mean."

"In the few days I've known you, I've given up fear and distrust. And it wasn't easy. For a lifetime, I've been carrying my diffidence like a shield to keep me safe and uncaring. Now it's gone. I'm free, but I can be hurt."

"By people like Jason?"

"That was a pinprick. There's only one person who can really wound me." His hand reached out, lightning-quick, to stroke the firm line of her jaw. One finger traced her lips as he said, "That's the girl next door. You were here all the time, and I never saw you."

Their conversation was growing too close for Crystal's comfort. She stepped away and aimed for home. "People change. Cities change. Only the mountains remain forever."

He fell into step beside her. "The mountains are constantly transforming. The level of streams rises and falls. The aspen turn gold and shed their leaves. Snow falls." He took her arm and turned her toward him. "Will you ever change as I have? Will you trust me, Crystal?"

She remembered his conversation with his secretary, his political aspirations, his stutter. There were all these many parts that made the man, and a thousand other faces she had never seen. How could she trust what she did not know? How could she place him above the dear aspirations that she'd followed for so long? "Change is always possible," she admitted. "If I didn't believe that, I wouldn't be a therapist."

"Do therapists change?"

She carefully freed herself from his grasp. The pressure of his hand on her arm melted her defenses, and she briskly fought her way back to a world she could understand. "One thing is constant. Time. And we have an appointment in ten minutes. We'd better make tracks."

They left the shadow of the golden dome and strode silently to the northeast. Crystal searched for a safe topic, uncomfortably aware that a discussion of their relationship could take hours. Even a lifetime. She only had minutes to spare. "I know your father's side of the family were homesteaders, but was your mother a native?"

He walked silently for a few paces, feigning acute interest in an orange and yellow border of geraniums planted beside the sidewalk. The subject of family relationships had once again been opened, and Crystal wondered at his reluctance to speak.

He seemed to make a conscious decision, signaled

by a slight nod of his head and almost imperceptible straightening of his shoulders. "My mother was a Radcliffe-educated Easterner who came West for the skiing and fell in love with the mountains."

"It must have been difficult for her to make the adjustment," Crystal probed lightly. "Denver must have seemed crude and unpolished."

"You obviously don't know my mother," he said in a tone that was tinged with bitter affection. "She creates her own environment. The very mountains were reshaped to her whim."

"Explain please."

"Our ranch house in the foothills was not, as you pointed out, the epitome of sophistication, but mother loved the indigenous roughness. For as long as I can remember, she ended every evening with a long walk in the hills. There were only two eastern habits she pined for—tennis and rose gardens. So she laid out her tennis courts in the back forty, bulldozed a section perfectly flat, and surrounded it with wild roses and grass that was sheer agony to water."

"Whom did she find to play with her?"

"Everybody." His lips twisted in a grimace that was half smile and half frown. Crystal found it impossible to deduce whether he adored or resented his mother. "It was not unusual to find our cowhands sprinting across the fields in tennis whites. And she beat most of them. Needless to say, her ideas lent an air of unreality to our ranch life."

Though Crystal's family had been city dwellers, she had grown up with the cowboy image. She knew them to be rough men whose boots seemed welded onto their feet. Their faces were carved from aged oak, timelessly chiseled by constant exposure to wind and sun. It was totally incongruous to imagine cowboys clad in Adidas and tennis shorts. Luke's mother must have had a will of iron.

He took the words from her mouth. "Mama was a tough old bird. Still is. Like your father, she's decided that Denver is too tame for a year-round existence. Right now she's in China, probably practicing her backhand against the Great Wall."

"I do admire her for one thing," Crystal mused. "You mentioned before that she taught you to cook. Most little boys can't boil water."

"I was never most little boys," Luke said, rather too quickly. "Not only can I cook and sew enough to get by, but I can horseback ride English and Western style. I can diaper a baby. Know first aid. And I play a real mean game of tennis."

"She must be proud of you, Luke."

They passed a row of ornate gingerbread-trimmed houses that had recently been restored to their former glory. Crystal waved to a white-haired lady who diligently trained her hose on a vegetable and flower garden.

When Luke finally replied, his low voice could not completely obscure the pain and disappointment. "I don't know if she's proud or not. Her standards are very high."

"Offhand, I would have to say that you should exceed any mother's reasonable expectations." She thought of Everett's mother, her black eyes brimming with tears, but still proclaiming her son's intelligence. "You've attained some professional renown. Your future prospects are absolutely golden. You're fit. You dress fairly well." She teased to soften her praises, "At least, you can tie your own shoes."

"But I still stutter."

Crystal had had enough psychological training to recognize the symptoms of Luke's fear, a condition that had probably complicated his relationship with women as he compared them all to his strong-willed mother. No wonder he was still unmarried. Here was yet another side to Luke Todhunter. Though it would take years of analysis to discover what made him tick, even an amateur like Crystal could deduce that some of his stuttering problem was rooted in a fear of failing his mother's expectations. "What would it take for you to be a success to your mother?"

"Not much." As he sauntered along the sidewalk, Crystal noticed that he stepped on every crack. "The presidency of the United States, something like that."

"Is that the real reason you're running for political office?"

"Maybe, but I don't think so." He fixed his eyes on her features in a significant glance. "I believe I've outgrown this love-hate thing with dear mama. Her approval and disapproval doesn't matter so much as my need to prove to myself that this stutter won't limit me. I told you before that I wanted to be a trial lawyer, and that's always been an impossible dream."

"Not so. Look at all the progress you've made in a few short days," she pointed out as they turned onto her street. Their path swerved to avoid a sprinkler. "You can practice any kind of law you want."

"Too complicated," he said with slow resignation. "I'd have to get you to kiss me before every speech, and most judges would frown on that particular courtroom behavior."

"Wait a minute. I thought we surpassed that obstacle. I didn't need to kiss you today."

"In front of a bunch of kids," he said disparagingly.

"If anything, that was the worst situation you could possibly encounter. You said yourself that little Jason awakened all your childhood memories."

He held open the wrought-iron gate to Crystal's yard. Honeysuckle vines scented the air with sweet fragrance as they proceeded up the walk. "You will be there tomorrow, won't you?" he suddenly asked. "When I have to face the town meeting?"

Crystal chose her words diplomatically. She refused to be Luke's crutch. If he was to live up to the incredibly high standards set by his mother, he must succeed in his own right. "As your therapist, I will be there. To observe. I'll sit in the audience to take notes for our session afterward."

"That's not enough," he said. "I want you with me onstage. I refuse to make a fool of myself like I did today."

"How could you say you were foolish? You were warm and kind and sharing. The children loved you."

"They love Porky Pig, too, but I don't think they'd vote for him."

As she fumbled through her vast handbag for her front door keys, he lifted her chin and searched her face. "Humor me, Crystal. I need all the help I can get."

Her heart flew to her throat and speech failed her. No matter how vehemently she denied her attraction for him, no matter how much she tried to play the objective therapist, the physical evidence was irrefutable. His every touch was like the warm air currents from the mountains that came at night to melt the winter's snow. She could refuse him nothing, but was forced to hold back everything—or accept the death of her own ambitions and professionalism. She turned her eyes away from his face. "No, Luke. I'm setting the conditions. No more kiss therapy. Remember in the mountains? You said you were a man of your word. Now, keep your promise."

She extracted the keys from her purse and fitted them into the lock. "Good afternoon, sir. I have another appointment."

His grip on her arm was surprisingly strong and insistent. Crystal recalled his plot to be gone from his office for the rest of the day. She knew this moment was a test between his will and hers.

Yet, when she faced him, it was not a dominating manipulative, macho male that stared through his deep-blue eyes. A forelock of blond hair fell across his forehead. Hurt was evident in his guileless expression that seemed to accuse. How could she be so cruel? Couldn't she see that he needed her?

She addressed his wordless pose. "Stop it, Luke. It doesn't become a powerful politician to look like a drowned puppy. I have no choice. Please excuse me."

He dropped her arm and sauntered to the porch swing. "I'll wait."

"We are through for the day." She stormed to his side and gave the wooden swing a violent jerk. "Go back to your office."

"Is this the way you treat all your clients?" He scooped up Rorschach the cat who had appeared from nowhere to nestle lovingly round his ankles. "I'm speaking to you as a therapist. I'm uncomfortable about the big speech tomorrow. I need another session."

"I won't be free until tomorrow morning. Perhaps we can make an appointment for noon."

"I won't let you skip lunch."

"As a client, my eating habits are none of your concern."

"But they are. I don't want my therapist keeling over from starvation. However, I think we can make a deal."

"Swell." She sighed, then flopped down next to him on the swing, sending it into motion. "Well, let's hear it, Mr. Lawyer."

"If you refuse to indulge in the highly successful kiss therapy, you've got to give me a substitute. Explain to me why the touch of your lips releases my lifelong stutter."

"That's fair enough," she agreed, although suspicious. "If that's all you want, you're being unusually reasonable."

He spread his hands. "For a conniving lawyer, I'm a pretty nice guy."

She marshaled her thoughts, a process that was common for a student on her way to a doctoral degree. Her reply was couched in professional terms. "Your stutter is stress related. When you appear before a group, your larynx tightens in response to that stress, causing a laryngospasm. And I would like to point out that your problem is extremely common. Public speaking is rated as the number one most threatening situation."

"I know people who thrive on it."

"But you hang around with lawyers, don't you? Average citizens are not normally given to making a public spectacle of themselves. The relevance of kiss therapy is this. When your mind is taken off the circumstance, you are free momentarily from that stress. Like substitution behavior."

"Why doesn't it come back later in the speech?"

"Because I happen to be a great kisser," she grinned. "Actually, it's because once you have conquered the stutter, your confidence level is heightened. Initial speech is the problem for most stutterers. Get past the introductory remarks, and you're home free."

"Then, there *is* a rational basis for kiss therapy," he said with a persuasive grin. "I'm not completely out of order to request that treatment."

"You are. And I won't. What we need to do is find another behavior to lower your stress level."

Crystal realized that she had just explained herself into another therapy session before his big speech tomorrow night, but she refused to give him the satisfaction of claiming her afternoon. "If you will come back at seven o'clock this evening, we'll try to discover another, more acceptable stimulus."

"It's a date."

"No," she corrected. "It's an appointment."

"I'll wait right here." He patted the wooden slats of the porch swing. "Maybe you'll be finished early, and I can treat you to dinner."

"I can't believe that a busy lawyer doesn't have something more productive to do with his time than camp on my doorstep. I'm sure I'll be busy until seven."

"I cleared my schedule for the afternoon, and even as we speak my secretary is probably breaking out the champagne for a celebration of her freedom."

Crystal remembered his phone call at the Children's Museum. "You're not a mean boss, are you?"

"Lately, I've been rather hard to live with." He gestured at their conflicting wristwatches. "Is that seven o'clock your time or mine?"

"Does five minutes make a difference?"

"When you've waited as long as I have, five minutes is an eternity."

8

HER CUPBOARDS WERE BARE. Her refrigerator stood virtually empty. There wasn't even milk to pour over the crumbled remains of dry cereal. Crystal kicked the refrigerator door closed and swore softly. A trip to the grocery store would easily solve her problem, but Crystal's shiny blue Volkswagen bug was parked in front by the curb. There was no way she could sneak past the handsome sentinel who still waited on the porch swing. "I'm a prisoner in my own house," she groaned.

He hadn't been completely immovable in his self-imposed guard duty. Between her appointments, Crystal glanced through the front window and was oddly disappointed to find the porch vacant. Yet by the end of her session Luke was back.

Now it was just past six o'clock. She peeked through the lace curtains in her sun room. He still had not moved.

During his absence, he'd changed from his business suit to a porch-sitting outfit of tennis shorts and T-shirt. Her gaze lingered on his long, muscular legs. She read the legend on his gold shirt: *Stop the Dam.* The black letters furled interestingly across the planes of his muscular chest. His brow furrowed with concentration as he read, but it was not a law brief or textbook that held his attention. Rather, he held a pa-

perback with a lurid cover. As Crystal tilted her head
to see the title, he caught her watching and waved.

Much chagrined, she closed the curtains and headed
for her near-empty pantry. After another survey of her
scanty food supply, she juggled her options: stubborn-
ness versus capitulation.

Even though she would be nearly an hour early for
their seven o'clock appointment, she had to eat. She
flung open the door and confronted Luke.

"Now your watch is really fast," he said, marking
his place in the book he'd been reading. Rorschach
was cuddled on his lap, and Luke Todhunter looked
for all the world as though he belonged on her front
porch.

"I'm going out to dinner," Crystal stiffly replied.
"I'll be back in time for our therapy session."

"I have an alternative."

"I don't want to hear it." Her irritation mounted.
What right had he to look so comfortable? She was
still dressed in her bright Children's Museum clothing and felt wilted by the day's labors.

"Brie, pâté and croissants," he said temptingly.
"Red wine from my private cellar. Flowers from FTD."

She eyed the hoard he had compiled beside the
swing: a grocery bag from the Deli Marv, a bottle and
a profusion of amber roses. A rush of pleasure de-
fused her hostility. Flowers always made her sigh,
and she was an avowed devotee of the nearby delica-
tessen. Still, she trained her features into a severe expression. "This is not standard procedure between
client and therapist, Todhunter."

"Consider it an apple for the teacher." He gathered
the flowers and presented her with a huge bouquet of
three dozen blooms.

Introducing
Harlequin Temptation™

Have you ever thought
you were in love
with one man...only
to feel attracted to another?

Exclusive Harlequin home subscriber benefits!

- CONVENIENCE of home delivery
- NO CHARGE for postage and handling
- FREE *Harlequin Romance Digest* ®
- FREE BONUS books
- NEW TITLES 2 months ahead of retail
- A MEMBER of the largest romance fiction book club in the world

GET **FIRST IMPRESSIONS** FREE AS YOUR INTRODUCTION TO NEW *Harlequin Temptation* ™ PLUS A FREE TOTE BAG!

® No one touches the heart of a woman quite like Harlequin

YES, please send me FREE and **without obligation** my *Harlequin Temptation* romance novel, *First Impressions* and my FREE tote bag. If you do not hear from me after I have examined my FREE book, please send me 4 new *Harlequin Temptation* novels each month as soon as they come off the press. I understand that I will be billed only $1.75 per book (total $7.00). There are no shipping and handling or any other hidden charges. There is no minimum number of books that I have to purchase. In fact, I may cancel this arrangement at any time. The FREE tote bag and *First Impressions* are mine to keep as a free gift, even if I do not buy any additional books.

142 CIX MDCZ

Name

Address   Apt. No.

City   State/Prov.   Zip/Postal Code

Signature (If under 18, parent or guardian must sign.)

Signature (If under 18, parent or guardian must sign.)
This offer is limited to one order per household and not valid to present *Harlequin Temptation* subscribers. We reserve the right to exercise discretion in granting membership. Offer expires February 28, 1985. PRINTED IN U.S.A

Get this romance novel and tote bag
FREE as your introduction to new

Harlequin Temptation ™

◁ See exciting details inside.

"Rather an elaborate bribe," she admitted, burying her nose in the roses' fragrance. How long had it been since anyone had given her flowers? She'd forgotten how it felt to be treasured. The silken petals reflected a golden glow in her eyes. "I don't suppose you picked up smoked oysters, did you?"

"And mustard sardines."

"Those crunchy little crackers?"

He wiggled his eyebrows and nodded.

"How did you know all my favorites?" she asked, her mouth beginning to water.

"A few leftovers in your kitchen one night, and a quick interview with Marv at the deli." He picked up the bag and the wine. "Marv was delighted that you had a date."

"Let's not make this into more than it is," she chided, sweeping into the house with her giant bouquet. "Call it a catered appointment."

Despite Crystal's assertion, they conducted very little therapy that evening. Wine and conversation flowed in pleasant ripples. They laughed together and slurped oysters and licked soft cheese from sticky fingers. Even when they left the kitchen table for the office, no therapy intruded on their camaraderie. Her home was too redolent with the scent of roses to be conducive to concentration.

Still, Luke remained faithful to his promise. He made no attempt to reenact kissing therapy. Instead, they bonded in friendship, enjoying each other and revealing private memories and dreams that created an intimate aura.

When Crystal's eyes strayed guiltily to her wristwatch, Luke took the hint. "You don't have another appointment, I hope."

"Only with my books. I've got to rewrite several paragraphs on my dissertation to accommodate new research."

"Are you nervous about your studies?"

"That's a mild term for my feelings," she admitted. "Borderline hysterical is more like it. I've got a bad case of academic anxiety."

His expression was entirely sympathetic. "I felt the same way in law school."

She fiddled with a long curl of auburn hair, and the twin worry lines appeared between her eyes. "I know it's irrational, but I keep thinking I'll fail, that something awful will prevent me from getting my degree."

He rested his fingertips on her temples and massaged gently. "I understand. You have four copies of your dissertation all hidden in different places so that in case of fire your work won't be destroyed."

"How did you know?" she murmured, feeling the tension being drawn from her.

"It's not unusual. Academic anxiety, as you called it."

Lazily, his leathery hands slid to the nape of her neck and continued the massage. Her head lolled forward.

She marveled at the wondrous power in his strong hands. Sometimes their mere touch excited her beyond imagining. Now, they gave her peace, surcease from the hectic daily grind. Without thinking, she assumed a stomach-down pose on the long sofa to give him access to her whole back.

He kneaded the taut muscles until they became smooth and pliant. "I do understand, Crystal. That's why I'm willing to accept your terms and to wait." He traced the line of her backbone. "And now, I'll bid you good night. I know you have work to do."

His considerate attitude made him irresistible. She rolled to her back. Through heavy-lidded eyes, she saw a friend, a man who could accept her ambitions. She wanted him to stay, but knew this was not the time. This companionable evening was proof of a deep bond between them. "Thank you, Luke. I've enjoyed this."

"When do I see you tomorrow? For therapy."

"I'm swamped. Why don't we meet just before the town meeting."

"In Golden. At Foss's Drugstore."

"Only if I can order a cherry Coke."

"I seem to be making a career of feeding you." He laughed. "Is the way to your heart through your stomach?"

"I'm an egghead, remember? You'll have to use a more intellectual approach."

"Next time I'll grease the wheels with Kant and Schopenhauer."

She followed him to the door and watched as the light from a corner streetlamp lit his way to his car. The night air was gentle, caressing. Even in the heart of the city, the hum of cicadas could be heard. Sensations of peace and contentment suffused Crystal Baxter. After a clear-headed bout with the books, she carried Luke's memory to her soft down pillow.

THE NEXT AFTERNOON at five o'clock, she aimed her Volkswagen toward Golden. The August sun blistered even as it waned. Blaring car horns punctuated the hot, dusty drive and heat waves rose from the highway.

The jacket of her mint-green suit lay wrinkled across the passenger seat, and the thin white cotton shirt stuck to her sweating back. Crystal's day had been full of frustrating endeavors and petty irritations.

As she entered Foss's Drugstore, she pushed a wave of damp hair from her moist forehead. She was sticky and frazzled and touchy. Yet, as soon as she spied Luke, she realized that her weary annoyance was a light burden compared to his state of mind.

He was frayed to the heightened edge of panic. His normally tan complexion was ashen. Tension constricted him like a coiled spring.

The town meeting was less than two hours away.

As Crystal watched him, a dull ache grew within her. She forgot her own worries and assumed the pain-filled panic he so obviously felt. All the jostling bustle of the drugstore and the neat rows of bottles and boxes and tubes faded before her weary eyes. The only clarity was Luke Todhunter, the man who needed her so desparately.

She forced herself to project calmness and prepared to give him all her strength. With a bright smile, she slid into the orange leatherette booth opposite him. "I'll have Dom Perignon, please."

"Let me summon the garçon." He responded to her humor in kind, but the effect was stiff and unnatural as he waved to a perky waitress. "Thank God you're here, Crystal."

"Where else would I be?" Her light tone disguised her deep concern. She would have to act quickly if she hoped to relax him enough to speak. Studying the tremor of his hands as he crumpled a plastic straw and noting the reflex clenching of his jaw, she recognized the emergency he had spoken of in their first encounter.

"Let's practice the air-flow technique," she said calmly.

"Here?"

"Why not? You can use that pink row of Pepto-Bismol as your audience."

He started the now-familiar introduction. "People of Jefferson County, you should be proud." He flipped through a huge stack of note cards.

"Wait, Luke. When you spoke to the group at my office, you didn't use cards, and you were very effective," she reminded him, hoping to boost his confidence with the remembered success. "Why are you reading your speech?"

"These are just some statistics." He shrugged. "In case I forget something."

She took the stack of five-by-eight cards. The text of his speech was written word-for-word in a scrawling hand. "These include everything but questions from the audience."

Ruefully, he showed her a section marked "probable questions."

"Why?" she questioned. "You don't need these. You're an expert on every facet of Coyote Creek Dam."

"I need every aid I can get." He convulsively grabbed the note cards from her. A nervous tic caused his right eye to blink and the eyebrow to raise involuntarily. "When I think of all those faces, those eyes staring, I'm scared, Crystal."

She winced. She hadn't expected him to be so devastated. Her judgment as a therapist had become clouded by her personal relationship with Luke.

Could this be the same man who had brought her brie and roses and chatted easily into the night? Why hadn't she foreseen this reaction?

"Will you be there?" he hoarsely croaked. The wooden expression on his blanched face described the lonely terror of a hunted beast. "You will be backstage, won't you?"

"I'll be anywhere you want me." She reached across the Formica tabletop to soothe his trembling hands. "In case you hadn't noticed, I care about you a lot."

"You're picking one hell of a time to tell me, Crystal." A tiny chuckle died on his lips. "There's nothing I can do about it right now."

"You can care back," she suggested, squeezing his hands. "That's what friends are for."

"Friends?" he said absently. "Is that what we are?"

"Very good friends. Yin and Yang. Laurel and Hardy." She denied the impulse to offer more intimate affection. Foss's Drugstore was hardly the appropriate setting to declare a relationship far beyond friendship.

"What about Romeo and Juliet? Lancelot and Guinevere? Clark Gable and Carole Lombard?"

"All those mythical, dead figures," she commented. "Why is it that to be truly romantic, somebody has to die? Do you know who I'd rather be? One half of Ralph and Alice on the 'Honeymooners.'"

He lifted one leaden hand to tenderly stroke her cheek as he repeated Ralph the bus driver's favorite line. "Baby, you're the greatest."

She responded to his touch like a cat receiving a petting caress. Her hands clasped his and she firmly pressed her lips into his palm. "I believe in you, Luke."

"At least one of us does."

"I'm not joking."

"I didn't think you were." He reclaimed his hand. "But until you release me from my promises, I can't tell you how I feel." He paused, and a sly gleam edged the panic from his eyes. "I can't tell you how much you mean to me. I can't even tell you that I love you."

His face was now closer to its normal color, and the tremor in his hands was growing less noticeable. In her role as therapist, Crystal should have been gratified at the improvement in his condition, but her blushing reaction was purely personal. He loved her.

They had trespassed the therapist-client relationship once again, and—despite her resolutions—she was glad. In the harsh fluorescent glare of the drugstore booth, she saw the bewitching flicker of candlelight. The cacaphony of a jukebox seemed like violins.

While his anxiety level dropped, hers increased. She hadn't wanted to fall in love. She didn't have time. Yet, the selfless caring she felt for Luke could not be called by any other name. She even experienced his pain. She was willing to sacrifice her emotional stability for his well-being.

"You're so lovely." He leaned back in the booth while the waitress set her cherry Coke on the table between them. He said not another word, but his eyes spoke forbidden volumes.

For once, Crystal did not avert her gaze, but allowed herself the pleasure of responding to him. "Thank you, Luke."

What else could she say in return? *You're gorgeous, the sexiest hunk I've ever seen. I adore the way your hair falls across your forehead. I could stare at your tan, weathered face for an eternity.* How could she express the tumultuous emotions she felt? *I want you, care for you, love you.*

"What are you thinking?" he asked.

"Don't you know?"

"I'd rather hear you say it."

She took a deep breath before the inevitable declaration that would color her existence in rose and pastel hues. She knew the world would never be the same after she whispered those three small words that had stuck in her throat for so long. The importance of the moment paralyzed her. Seeking release for her words, her hands flew like wild butterflies, reaching for him.

Her gesture turned comic when her fluttering hand collided with the Coca-Cola glass. Ice chunks and carbonated liquid spilled across the table onto his lap, marking him with her still undeclared passion.

He leaped to his feet, swabbing the cola with flimsy paper napkins. "I know I was out of line," he said. "But you didn't have to literally throw cold water on me."

She yanked more napkins from the dispenser. His blue suit, a shade lighter than his eyes, was stained in a huge, embarrassing patch. "Better try to wash that out," she advised, limply.

"You're right. People will wonder what I've been up to." He stepped away from the booth, pausing only long enough to drop a light kiss on her forehead. "George Burns and Gracie Allen," he said.

When he returned, she saw with relief that the stained area was not discolored, only wet. She'd paid the bill and left the table to peruse the magazine rack nearby. Though she never purchased tabloids, their screaming headlines always enticed her. She looked up from an article about Siamese twins and held out the photo for him to see. "It could be worse. There could be two of me." She barely suppressed a giggle. "Then we could be the Three Stooges."

The music of his laughter cheered her. They had all but forgotten the important speech that would launch his new career as a politician. The appearance of a frantic Ms Baumann brought them back to harsh reality.

"There you are," the skinny woman with thick glasses and a clipboard stated unnecessarily. She stared pointedly at Luke's wet suit. "What happened?"

"Nothing that a few seconds in the August sun won't cure." Luke took Crystal's arm protectively and introduced her.

Ms Baumann's response was automatic. "Pleased to meet you." She bobbed a curt nod. "Are you ready, Mr. Todhunter? Everybody's waiting."

"Let me get my note cards."

Crystal produced a sodden stack of blurred cardboard from her purse. "Sorry."

"I'm not. You were right. I don't need idiot cards. All I need is you."

Crystal read the wintry change in Ms Baumann's expression. Luke's secretary wasn't blatantly disapproving. It was more like she had found the proper pigeonhole for her employer's new "friend."

Crystal straightened the lapels of her jacket and pulled her professional armor into place. She wasn't sure she liked the connotation of Ms Baumann's knowing leer. In fact, she positively despised it. "Shall we go? Your public awaits."

Ms Baumann lurched on skinny bird legs beside Luke. She referred to her clipboard to enumerate the dignitaries, the newspaper people and the TV reporters who would be present at the town meeting. "I don't know why we haven't done this before," she said excitedly. "This is wonderful exposure."

Crystal worried about the impact of Ms Baumann's VIP list on Luke's renewed confidence, but he seemed untouched by her chatter. All his attention was focused on Crystal's auburn hair and blushing cheeks. He held her hand as they strolled along the main street of Golden, pausing to read the gaudy sign that spanned the street: Welcome to Golden. Where the West Remains.

The small-town atmosphere of Foss's Drugstore and the five-and-dime and the neighborly gas station contrasted with the gigantic Coors Corporation located just beyond the next valley. Denim jeans and Western shirts were the rule despite the high-powered executive occupations of many of the inhabitants.

Luke commented on the incongruity and added, "With all the Coors people in the audience, it might get hostile. Their position on the dam is full speed ahead."

"You're talking to a member of the opposition, you know," Crystal reminded him.

"Still?"

"Absolutely. However, I am beginning to see your good points."

They entered the backstage area of the auditorium and were immediately surrounded by Luke's entourage. Fawning ladies and intense young men and a few cigar-smoking politicos surged around their candidate. Crystal was swept from his side by Ms Baumann for her own round of introductions as Luke's "friend." The polite handshakes and lack of interest implied that she was probably not the first woman to have been so displayed, and she felt cheapened.

These people obviously considered her one of the strange bedfellows made by politicians. Luke stood at the eye of this human tornado, and the faces around him seemed like anxious reflections in a house of mirrors. They weren't hostile toward her, merely uncaring. For a moment, she felt a powerful urge to proclaim her validity.

Ms Baumann outlined seating arrangements for the dignitaries who would share the stage with Luke, and Crystal heard his objection. "Ms Baxter will sit by my side."

"Oh no." Ms Baumann seemed inordinately puzzled. "The mayor of Golden is on one side and the president of the Jaycees is on the other."

Luke took her penciled sketch, scratched out the mayor and wrote in Crystal. As he handed it back, Ms Baumann said, "Well, how do we explain her? People will wonder who she is."

Luke smiled down at the small, auburn-haired woman beside him. "I'd like to say that she's my future w—"

Crystal whipped her head from side to side vehemently, and he amended. "She's my very good friend. No further explanation is necessary."

Crystal recognized the masterful side of Luke's personality coming to the fore. He was the demanding attorney who brooked no objection to his will. "If you don't mind," she heard herself saying, "I would rather be offstage."

"I don't want to hear arguments, Crystal. I need you to be close."

She had a disturbing premonition that he meant to kiss her before speaking—in front of all these people. Inwardly, she cringed. She hadn't studied all these years to be made into a public spectacle. "I won't go through with this, Luke."

He took her by the arm and marched her to a far corner. With his back shielding them and ensuring a small measure of privacy, he asked, "Why won't you sit with me onstage? It's a way of showing support. Nancy Reagan always sits with her Ronnie."

"That is not the same thing. Ronnie doesn't intend to give her a big smack on the lips before he goes to the podium."

"Sure he does, and people like it. Adds a little romance to his image. Besides, I want someone who I know is in my corner, up there on stage with me."

She gestured toward the throng of admirers. "You don't lack supporters, and that role doesn't suit me. I'm not a prim, sweet, political appendage who can stare for hours at the superstar candidate." She fluttered her eyelashes in a sarcastic impersonation of rapt attention.

"Listen, you can cross your eyes and pick your nose for all I care. I want you there beside me."

"At least political wives have the virtue of matrimony on their side. At least they are recognized as partners in the great man's career." She thoroughly resented the position he was forcing her to accept. Even if she made allowances for his nervousness, his attitude was almost bullying. "You're just using me, Luke."

"Of course I am," he said honestly. "And I hope you will feel free to use me. That's called sharing, Crystal."

"Not on my scorecard it isn't," she snapped. A hot anger sparked from her amber-flecked eyes. "It is emotional extortion."

"You always resort to multisyllable accusations when you're angry or upset. Did you know that?" His own displeasure grew evident. "Now, I won't put up with any more of this nonsense. You'll sit beside me, and that is that."

"Don't you dare treat me like some brainless chippie." Her voice quavered in full-fledged rage. "Get some other little honey to kiss you before you speak. It shouldn't matter which groupie you grope."

He grabbed her arm, and she felt the steely strength of the man. "Stop this," he commanded. "There is no reason for you to be acting like a spoiled brat. Dammit, I love you."

She pulled free and took a deep breath. She wanted nothing more than to escape from the auditorium, to run into the streets of Golden. Outside, the sun would be setting behind the hills. The sky would be rosy and peaceful. The cool whisper of evening would be rising. She drew sustenance from those mauve-tinted breezes to displace this angry wedge that separated them. Summoning her professionalism, she spoke as his therapist. "You have the skills necessary to speak effectively tonight. I believe in you. I believe in your ability, and I will do anything within reason to support you."

"Prove it," he challenged. "Be there for me. Sit by my side."

"I won't run out on you," she said through clenched teeth. "But the thought is very tempting."

She looked away from his granite-hard features. What was he trying to do? What had happened to the sensitive, tender Luke she loved? Her father would have said that a skunk doesn't show his true colors except in sunlight.

Luke obviously didn't reveal the stuff he was made of until a spotlight touched his thick head of blond hair. He didn't care about her feelings. All he wanted was someone to stroke his ego.

He touched her arm softly and said, "You know, Crystal, almost every time we've been in a group, you've controlled the situation. You ran the DSD meeting. You directed the kids at the museum. Now the shoe is on the other foot. This is my show, and I think that bothers you."

"I'm not your opponent." No matter what personal tumult she endured, it was her responsibility to encourage him. "I am your therapist, and I want you to succeed."

"But you don't want me calling the shots," he said. A trace of bitterness colored his voice. "As long as I'm a helpless stutterer, you can be my solace, but when I make the rules you want to quit the game."

"Calling the shots?" She erupted, forgetting duties and therapies and rules. "Ever since you first jammed your foot in my door, you've been running my life. There is no way I would ever call you helpless, and if you want someone to feel sorry for you, look someplace else because you're not getting any pity from me."

Her explosion succeeded where cautious therapeutic jargon had failed. The hurt and anger slipped from his face. "You're right."

A loud throat-clearing announced the presence of Ms Baumann. "Mr. Todhunter, it's time for you to take your place onstage. I've arranged for an extra chair for Ms Baxter."

"That won't be necessary." He straightened his cuffs. "Unless Ms Baxter prefers to sit with me?"

"No, thank you."

"Very well. I'm ready."

She watched him stride toward the light and was grateful for the dark solitude in the wings to cover her confusion. A whole other side of Luke Todhunter had been revealed to her, and she didn't know what to believe. Though he admitted that she was right, she was left feeling that he had the last word.

What did he want from her? A political wife? Someone to sit beside him on the podium and laugh at his jokes and applaud his brilliance? He must know by now that that was a person she could never be. She hated that identity, considered it a total waste of time. "And talent," she said aloud. "I'm a skilled person, one of the best in my field. I can't be happy as an adoring bystander."

She stopped abruptly. The realization hit her like a slap in the face. Bull's-eye. Luke had been on target when he said that she needed to be in control. She loved competition. It was so obvious that Crystal had overlooked that facet of her personality. Her goals. Her aims. Her knife-edged spirit was much to blame for this misunderstanding. Perhaps he knew her better than she knew herself.

In this auditorium, he was the unquestioned center of attention, and her ego had been slighted. How childish! She couldn't even suppress her ambitiousness for the one evening when he was making an important speech. She wasn't used to thinking of anyone but herself, and she fervently hoped that her insistence on getting her own way would not hurt him. If his stutter surfaced in this threatening setting, he would never be able to trust himself to speak again.

She walked slowly to the curtain at the front of the stage and peeked through the far edge. The auditorium was small, seating only three hundred people, but it was almost full. Would this audience witness the birth of a politician? Or his early demise? As Crystal watched, the lights dimmed. She moved to the area nearest the stage, thoughtlessly butting through the retinue of Todhunter supporters until she reached a position where he could see her.

The mayor of Golden made a laudatory and lengthy introduction, but Crystal only had eyes for the candidate. He was so handsome. His posture so correct. Only someone as close as she would notice his pallor and the tremor of his neatly folded hands.

She prayed for his success, sent heartfelt promises of eternal good behavior if only Luke could speak without stuttering. Her thoughtlessness rebuked her. If he failed, she would never forgive herself.

He stepped to the microphone. A hush fell. The bright glare of the TV camera flared to life. Luke gripped the podium. He tried to smile, but the effect was ghastly. He started, "P-p-people of J-jefferson C-c-county."

His jaw locked in pained agony. He took a deep breath. "You have r-r-reason to be p-p-proud."

He turned his gaze toward the wings. Unconciously, Crystal's hands twitched to summon him.

Into the microphone, he whispered, "P-p-please excuse me."

He purposefully strode to her side, ignoring the as-

tonished stares from his staff, their gasps of surprise
and their questions.

As soon as he was shielded from the audience by
the heavy velvet curtains, Crystal pulled the candidate into her arms. She kissed him with a zeal born of
deep, selfless caring and infused him with her own
strength. Her lips consumed him, fingers dug into his
back. She made him a part of herself and unlocked his
tongue with her own.

"I love you, Luke." Her tawny eyes blazed. "Now
go out there and give them hell. You can do it. You can
do anything."

It was a new man who relieved the mayor of
Golden at the podium. His baritone was smooth and
cool. His poise was perfection. "Sorry for the interruption," he said. "I had to have a private conference
with the president of the Luke Todhunter Fan Club."

The audience relieved their discomfort with a laugh.

"Sounded like you ate a frog," came a voice from
the front row.

Luke stepped around the podium, unhooking the
microphone as he walked. He squinted into the dark
auditorium. "Apparently, I've got another admirer."
He gestured to the backstage technicians. "Could we
have some light out here. I like to see who I'm talking
to."

The auditorium lights went on.

"That's better," he said, taking a casual perch on
the edge of the stage. "You know, I'm tired of politicians who tell people what to think. I shouldn't be
standing up here. You should. You're the ones who
make the decisions and live with the consequences.
Yours is the voice of government. To tell you the
truth, I didn't care who was elected or what they de-

cided until the folks in the State House decided to flood hundreds of the most beautiful acres on God's earth."

He continued in a gentle, conversational tone, and Crystal allowed herself to relax. Not a trace of a stutter marred his voice as he told the people that he cared about Jefferson County and about them and their children. He was better than eloquent. His sincerity rang true, and the audience was captivated. They laughed when he wanted them to laugh. When he described the proposed site for the dam, Crystal was sure that some wept for the natural splendor of the land.

He was going to be all right. It was his show, and he controlled it masterfully.

Quietly, Crystal left the auditorium.

9

CRYSTAL BAXTER HAD NEVER THOUGHT she was the type of woman who could fall in love. Her perspectives and opinions were carefully founded on rational thinking. Her relationships were never precipitous. Crystal was a looker, not a leaper.

Her other relationships with men had shown calm, sometimes curious acceptance. She had experimented with passion, but never plunged. Her feet were too firmly planted on the ground for her to fly. She was too smart, too clever, too busy to be swept into irrational realms of fancy.

Yet, as she sat alone in her rambling Victorian house, her mind persisted in replaying visions of Luke. She could not control the tingling sensations that left her light-headed and weak. There was Luke on the porch swing, Luke in the mountains dripping wet with diamond droplets of water clinging to his firm, hair-roughened chest, Luke in his custom-made business suit, easily manipulating Ms Baumann on the phone, Luke laughing, Luke nervous, Luke at the podium—a whole population of mystical, masculine, marvelous Lukes.

She had never before considered that love could be fun. It seemed that all the descriptions she'd read were tortured yearnings of star-crossed lovers. Did Romeo and Juliet ever share a good laugh? Yet that was the Luke she longed for most—the man who made her grin. She could hardly wait to be held in his arms and to hear the rumble of his laughter echo in his powerful chest.

Why had she run away? Crystal analyzed her flight and decided that there was not a good rationale. Perhaps she needed a safe haven, a respite from the topsy-turvy roller coaster where untapped emotions careened wildly out of control. She needed the time to think.

Her father used to say that once you've bought the ticket, you can't get off until the ride is over. Crystal had never dared before. She'd never sky-dived or soared. The only comparable sensation was the slalom course in skiing when she went so fast that there was no time to analyze the physical responses, only to react.

"And it's time for a break," she said to the many invisible Lukes that haunted her mind. "I need to clear my head."

In her bedroom, she flicked on the television. A summer rerun of "Dallas" showed the hapless Texans going through their machinations. *Those are the type of women who have mad, passionate affairs,* she thought. *Gorgeous and vulnerable and classy.*

She peered into the full-length mirror with its ornate, antique oak border. That mirror had watched Crystal grow from pinafore to lace. She stood before it in her blue kimono and slipped the silk from one slender shoulder. "Freckles," she said disapprovingly.

She ran her hand through the thick, auburn hair that had never learned to behave. Her clean-scrubbed face was too angular, not soft like those "Dallas" women. She peeped one long, supple leg through the front slit. "Definitely my best feature."

Her self-examination was interrupted by the ringing of the telephone. Crystal gave the mirror a sexy wink as she answered, instinctively knowing it was Luke. "Hello, handsome."

"That's a dangerous way to answer. How do you know I'm not an obscene caller?"

"I can always hope," she sighed. The timbre of his baritone sent ecstatic thrills through her body. "Your speech was excellent."

"What you heard of it," he said roughly. "Why the hell did you disappear?"

There was no mistaking the identity of this particular Luke Todhunter. This was macho Luke, probably clenching the telephone receiver in a white-knuckled fist.

"You're mad," she deduced.

"Of course I'm mad. I come off the stage expecting to find you, and instead Ms Baumann informs me that my friend is gone."

"Does it matter?"

"You don't need to ask that question, Crystal."

She decided that she preferred her imaginary Lukes to this hostile fellow. How dared he interfere with her dreams in such realistic tones!

His voice turned suspicious. "What's that I hear in the background? Do you have company?"

"Just an old friend." She stuck out her tongue at the video image of J.R. Ewing. "You might like him," she said dryly. "You two have a lot in common."

"There's a man at your house?"

"In my bedroom," she teased.

"And that's why you hurried off. You had a date."

Outrage was evident in his accusation, but Crystal refused to take him seriously. His assumptions were

ludicrous. Surely he knew her better than to think she
would declare love for him and then hedonistically
tumble into the arms of another man. She counted on
his sense of humor and turned the volume on the
television louder.

"And what a date." She chuckled. "I can turn him
on and off at will. He's around every Friday night,
and his name is...."

"I don't need to know his name. I don't need to
know anything else."

"Oh, Luke. Don't you get it? I'm pulling your leg."

"I can see what you're doing." His icy voice chilled
the telephone wires. "I assume our therapy appointment for tomorrow morning is a firm appointment,
Ms Baxter. I will see you then. Alone."

The receiver went dead. Crystal stared at it in hor-
ror as if the long, black cord was a deadly viper. How
dumb! She'd joked herself right out of his good
graces. Instead of a victory celebration for his tri-
umphant speech, she was condemned to spend this
Friday night in her separate cell practicing self-
flagellation.

She had wanted the time to think, not to mope. She
shook her head and growled at the telephone. It was
all the fault of Alexander Graham Bell and whoever
had invented the television. Electronics had frazzled
their affair. *Stand by. Technical difficulties.*

Ridiculous, she thought. *But easily patched up.*

She dialed his phone number and let it ring twelve
times before she hung up. Apparently he was still in
Golden, maybe even pursuing a victory celebration of
his own. That thought caused a twinge of panicky
jealousy akin to his irritation with her, and she understood the unreasonable anger a simple doubt

could create. The imagined picture of Luke in the arms of some willing political groupie left her glum and dispirited.

She shook off an impending depression and told herself that she was above leaping to erroneous conclusions. Crystal Baxter was not the sort of woman who wallowed in self-pitying introspection.

The NewsBreak on the television reinforced her fears. There was Luke, sitting on the edge of the stage and looking like every woman's dream lover. He was saying, "The natural heritage of our mountains must be preserved for future generations. Coyote Creek Dam must be defeated."

The chic brunette newscaster followed with her minianalysis. "And so, a bright new candidate throws his hat into the ring. More at ten."

The sound of the telephone made her jump. Maybe it was Luke calling back. She decided to level with him immediately. "Hello?"

"Crystal? This is Ginger. Did you see our Libra friend on television? I guess his first campaign speech went well."

Crystal flopped across her ivory chenille bedspread. "I guess so."

"Well, aren't you p-proud of yourself? Only a few days ago the man was inarticulate. You are a b-b-bona fide miracle worker."

Only ten days ago since she had first met him. It seemed forever.

"Crystal? Are you there?"

"Physically, yes." She rolled to her back. "But I'm totally exhausted."

"I didn't wake you, did I?"

"On a Friday night? Heavens no. I was just getting

ready to cruise the singles scene." She stared at the
ceiling fan and counted the lazy rotations. "Actually,
I've got a hot date with a cold dissertation."

Along with her claims to ESP and the nonsense
about astrological signs, Ginger actually was quite
perceptive. "You're depressed," she stated as fact.
"And I'm not going to guess how, what, when or
why."

Crystal murmured her thanks.

"I'm simply going to offer a bit of advice. Take the
evening off, dear. Read a good book—not a textbook—and drink a glass of wine. My own solution to
the kind of mood you're in is a hot fudge sundae, but
I'm sure you have healthier cravings."

Crystal thought of Luke, his lips and long legs and
muscular torso. "I've got cravings, all right."

"Then, indulge. I'll call in the morning. Don't forget to watch Luke on the ten o'clock news."

Crystal said goodbye and immediately redialed
Luke's number. He still wasn't home.

With a sigh, she decided to take Ginger's advice. A
good book, a jug of wine and...pizza. It made the
perfect antidote to depression. She called Mascaratti's
for a delivery.

A good book was next on her agenda. She went
downstairs and scanned her office shelves, finding
nothing but scholarly tomes and treatises. It had been
a long time since she treated herself to a good read,
and she wasn't prepared.

Her private library was no better. Filled with gilt-
lettered classics in leather bindings, the selection was
forbidding. She remembered the book with the lurid
cover that Luke had been reading on her porch swing

and went in search. In the kitchen, she located the latest mystery-thriller by John D. MacDonald. Perfect.

She poured a glass of leftover wine from the night before and settled into a comfortable chair to await the pizza man.

By chapter four, Crystal was engrossed. She treated herself to another glass of wine and dove back into the fast-paced narrative. When the doorbell sounded, it took a minute to recall that she had ordered a pizza with everything on it.

Carrying the book, she went to the door, wallet in hand. She peeped through the glass oval before opening. Luke Todhunter stood revealed in the porch light with a flat, white pizza box in his hand.

His blue eyes narrowed at the sight of Crystal in a kimono.

She swung open the door. "How much? Not including your tip." A wide grin curved her lips. Her wine-brightened eyes sparkled. She couldn't suppress her pleasure at seeing him. "Since when did you take a part-time job as a delivery man for Mascaratti's?"

"I pulled up at the same time as the pizza truck. Seems there's no unemployment problem with pizza delivery. The driver was easily bribed to let me take over his job."

"Won't you come in? I'd like to explain about my friend."

"You don't have to answer to me," he said defensively as he held his position on the porch. His earlier anger bubbled just below the surface, covered with a thin veneer of poise. "But I would like to meet the competition."

"I'm afraid that won't be possible. I didn't videotape him." Without a trace of humor lest he misunderstand again, she explained. "My boyfriend was J.R. Ewing. I was watching 'Dallas.'"

He looked doubtful. "I heard voices."

"That you did. It was background noise from the TV."

"The television?" he said incredulously.

She nodded. "Aren't you ashamed of yourself?"

"It's not *all* my fault," he snorted self-righteously. "I didn't expect an academic type like you to be watching low-brow, nighttime soap operas."

"Surprise," she announced. "I'm as happily tasteless as the rest of the world."

Luke prowled the porch with his eyes as though he expected J.R. himself to materialize from the shadows. "Are you sure it was only the television?"

"Well, not exactly. I have another beau. Someone you know." She held up the paperback book. "John D. MacDonald. Are you jealous?"

"I'm jealous of anything and anyone who touches you. I want you all for myself, my lovely Amber Lady."

Her joy at hearing his silly endearment surpassed rational understanding. "Then, get in here. We're letting in the moths."

He carefully set the pizza on the hall table. "Were you going to eat this all by yourself?"

"It's only a ten incher," she shrugged. "Besides, I'm indulging, taking some advice from Ginger. Remember her, from the stutterers group?"

"The short woman with gypsy bracelets?"

"That's Ginger, and if she were here, she would want me to wish you well on your campaign. According to the NewsBreak, you are a bright new candidate."

"Thanks to you." He took the book and wallet from her hands and placed them on top of the pizza box. "May I return your therapeutic kiss?"

Her hands fit on his waist. "You may."

Slowly and deliciously his lips descended to hers for a sweet exploration. He lingered there, adoring the softness and whispering to the core of her sensual being in the universal language of desire.

They melted together, savoring the fulfillment that was yet to come. His breath tickled her ear. "You taste like red wine."

"Would you like some?"

"I'd rather get drunk on the nectar of you."

He scooped her into his arms and started up the stair. A lover's sense of direction led him directly to the bedroom door where a soft amber light glowed from the bedside lamp bathing the feminine room in gentle shadow. He gazed down at his precious burden.

Her arms twined around his neck, and her head rested against his chest. Demure, brown eyelashes formed twin crescents on her freckled cheeks. Her silky sleeves fell back to reveal the tender curve of her slender arms. Through the slit in her kimono, her long legs were fully revealed.

His voice caught in his throat. "You're perfect, Crystal. The most beautiful woman I've ever seen."

"Nobody's perfect," she automatically corrected as she opened her gold-flecked eyes. "But some of us are very, very good."

With as much grace as she could muster in her awkward position, she yanked back the bedspread. He lowered her gently, taking exquisite care to arrange her limbs with arms spread over her head and legs long and straight on the pink flowered sheets. For a long moment, he simply stared before taking his place beside her on the bed.

With languid motion, she ran her hand down his light blue shirt. Her fingers undid the top button, then the next and the next until the thick, curling pelt was bared to her touch.

They shared the elegant pleasure of her tactile quest. She twirled her fingers in the mat of brown hair and lightly raked his sensitized skin. She discovered the hard, masculine nipple and teased its erogenous surface with her fingernail.

"Take off your shirt," she commanded huskily, and he complied.

"Now it's my turn," he threatened.

"No fair," she protested. "All I'm wearing is my kimono and panties."

"All's fair in love."

He untied the wide sash and slid the silken, teal-blue material from her so she lay uncovered to his electric gaze. He praised her body with his lips, caressed her with his tongue from the hollow of her throat to the lace edge of her panties and beyond as slowly he glided the wispy garment down her legs. His tongue described fiery circles that unloosed savory ecstasies and forbidden pleasures.

Crystal had been loved before, but never with such lambent tenderness, as though her body was a fine instrument to be tuned only by a master. His feathery touch grew insistent as the tempo increased. Her swollen breasts rose and fell with the rapid breaths of passion. She desired him, yet wished to prolong this excruciating torture for an eternity. She writhed under the incredible ministrations of his lips and tongue, finally arching toward him, unable to hold herself back. She drew him to her pulsing lips for a final, hard kiss, then demanded, "Take off your trousers."

"Would you like to help?"

"No." She didn't trust her trembling fingers. "Stand right there and take them off."

He sat on the edge of the bed and removed shoes and socks.

"Hurry, Luke." She playfully clawed at his back.

"Patience, my love. All good things are worth waiting for."

She propped herself on one elbow to watch him strip. The belt was unbuckled. Pants unzipped. He slid the waistband lower and lower and stripped his slacks and jockey shorts with a flourish.

Crystal had never been so wantonly direct in her perusal of a nude male form, but she wanted to know Luke intimately and completely. She wanted to touch the tiny scar on his left thigh, to massage the inside of his elbow, to kiss the arch of his foot and the palm of his calloused hand. His body, shamelessly revealed to her, was the most exciting and wonderful sculpture Crystal had ever seen. She couldn't wait to experience every inch of him, and her lips puckered for a low, appreciative whistle.

Laughter rose from his belly and shook him with pure delight. His teeth were white and perfect. He settled beside her on the queen-sized, four-poster bed. "Are you this uninhibited with all your clients?" he asked as his huge, rough hand completely covered her breast and teased the roseate peak.

Her wide, amber eyes were guileless. "Only with the hard-core cases, the ones who drive me mad."

"What about this?" His hand descended the velvet swell of her stomach and hips and fondled the auburn triangle of hair below. "Does this drive you crazy?"

"Oh God, Luke. You know it does."

Once again, his lips caressed her, nuzzling into the center of her soft, moist hair.

Crystal poised on the brink of sensuous madness, every nerve tingling, every pore crying out for his touch. He penetrated her satin longing with his tongue, then eased himself onto her body.

The full pressure of his virile hardness against her willing flesh propelled her to ecstasies hitherto unknown. She wrapped her arms convulsively around his back, her legs around his torso.

When his hard shaft pierced her, Crystal couldn't help crying out at the sheer perfection of their mating. No words existed for the dynamic rapture she felt.

"More," she whispered as they ascended the frenzied pinnacle of abandon in rhythmic strokes. She knew instinctively that this moment transcended all others. She nurtured the flames that engulfed her in sweet torment. "Slower," she gasped. "Go slower, Luke."

"Like this?" He coursed through her, deeply, sending shivers of dear agony through her whole being. He withdrew, then reentered and thrust again. "Is this what you want?"

"Oh yes, more," she exhorted, her untapped sensuality making her greedy.

"Any other instructions?" he breathed hoarsely.

"I'm a therapist," she said between shuddering gulps of oxygen. "I just wanted you to get it right."

"Is this right?"

In answer, she laced her legs with his and increased

the velocity to a wild crescendo. Finally, spent, she felt herself floating on fleecy white clouds. Her grasp loosened. She was nearly unconscious, marvelously euphoric. Arms fell loosely to the bed. Her legs sprawled beneath him as slowly, beautifully, she returned to earth.

He rolled from her, thoroughly sated and utterly relaxed. His body was covered with a film of perspiration. His arm still cradled her head. "I love you, Crystal."

She cuddled closer to him, loving the musky scent he exuded and the roughness of his chest hair against her cheek. "After what we've just been through," she managed to say, though her mouth was dry as cotton, "that's a bit redundant."

She heard the rumble of laughter in his chest.

"Always the scholar," he said. "Redundant? Couldn't you respond like a normal woman? Just tell me you love me."

"I'm not a normal woman," she said with absolute smugness. "That's why you are intrigued."

"If normal means average, you're surely not that," he agreed. "You're much, much better. Gifted. A-plus. Where did you learn to make love?"

"I'm not a virgin, if that's what you're getting at."

"How many times?" His voice was lightly mocking, but she sensed an undercurrent of petulance. *Every man likes to be the first,* she thought, and decided to tease. "How many times?" she repeated. "You mean exactly?"

"Precisely."

She stared at the ceiling fan and drew her eyebrows into an expression of intense concentration. She made a great show of counting on her fingers.

"You can use your toes if you need to," he said with exasperation. "Let's make it easier. How many times this year?"

"Calendar year? Or from August to August?"

"More than ten? Less than fifty?"

His banter was ruined by a pleading note, and she leveled with him. "Once. On my twentieth birthday."

"Once?" He was incredulous. "You're a semivirgin."

"I hope that doesn't disappoint you." She wrinkled her nose. "It wasn't much of a learning experience, either. More like a botched, curious experiment."

"Did you love him?"

"What is this? Twenty Questions? When do I get my turn?"

He reclined on the pillow, hands folded beneath his head. "Ask anything you'd like."

Crystal didn't want to hear about his other conquests. Though she was sure their lovemaking would not suffer in comparison, she banished his prior loves from her bedroom. No Molly or Susie or Katie would intrude on the golden light from her bedside lamp. Her eyes caressed the length of his body. "Has anyone ever told you that you're beautiful?"

"Not recently." He shifted uncomfortably under her scrutiny. "Was that your only question?"

"I guess so." She trailed her fingers along the pattern of his chest hair and again devoured him with her eyes. "You really are a ten, aren't you Luke?"

"I never measured." He caught her hand and carried it to his lips. "Do you love me, Amber Lady?"

"Maybe only a nine-and-a-half," she giggled. "You do have this little scar on your leg."

"I can see that I'm going to have to force it out of

you," he said with teasing ominousness. "Do you love me?"

He stroked her satiny skin. His muscular thigh moved against hers, and her lightning response was uncontrollable anticipation.

"Stop it, Todhunter. I can't do this again." She slapped his venturing hand away.

Swiftly, he lowered his body onto hers, effectively pinning her on the bed. She wriggled beneath his weight. "Do you love me?"

"You can't be serious? Aren't you tired?"

"Tell me, Crystal."

She struggled, though she had no real wish to escape the searching caress that molded the curve of her waist and glided to the wetness below. She thrashed against him, excited by her helplessness and suddenly willing to scale the heights of passion again. The re-emergence of desire shocked her. She had thought her body incapable of rising from the utter peace he had delivered earlier.

His lips hovered a centimeter away from hers. His breath was warm and soothing. "Do you love me, Crystal?"

"I'll tell you later," she purred.

THE SECOND AFTERMATH of lovemaking was even more perfect than the first, but Crystal had no wish to pursue a third assault. She hugged the large man who lay so still beside her and whispered, "I do love you, Luke. I adore you. I care for you. I love you."

"That's better," he yawned. "Sleepy?"

She assessed her feelings, enumerated the many sensations that crowded her mind. "Mostly, I'm hungry. Care for some cold pizza?"

"Do you deliver?' he asked lazily.

"Isn't that an unnecessary question?'

She climbed from the bed and padded down the stairs, still naked. Grabbing the pizza box and the jug of red wine, she scampered back to the bedroom and found it vacant.

The pulsing sounds of the shower told her Luke's whereabouts. Crystal briefly toyed with the idea of joining him, but decided that the night had been too fulfilling already. She donned her kimono and sat cross-legged on the bed sweetly scented by their passion. She flipped open the lid of the pizza box and dug into the thick, mozzarella-laden crust. Her voracious appetite was not surprising in light of her prior exertions.

"Better hurry, she shouted over the roar of the shower. "I won't promise to save you a piece."

When he rejoined her with only a towel wrapped around his waist, she felt a warm pleasure. He was her man simply and completely. She blessed the stutter that had brought them together.

"Your place or mine?" he said.

"Since we're here, we might as well stay," she replied with some confusion. "Luke, what are you talking about?"

"This is more convenient," he said, as his eyes wandered to the high ceilings and wide casement windows. "I only have a condominium in town, and the ranch is too far to commute from."

"Would you like to explain?" A long thread of cheese dangled from the pizza and she munched her way to the end.

"Isn't it obvious? Come on, Amber Lady, use that

giant brain of yours." He favored her with a cheerful smile. "We belong together."

All sorts of objections rose in her mind. She hadn't bargained on so complete a commitment, so soon. "You're kidding, right?"

He cupped her face in his hands. "Don't refuse me. I want to be with you every morning when I wake up."

She wriggled away and lifted the wine bottle to her lips. After a hearty swig, she apologized, "I only brought one glass." She filled the long-stemmed glassware and handed it to him."

"You're stalling," he accused.

"Well, you don't really expect to move in, do you? Right now?"

"Why not? We're compatible. We're friends. We can laugh together." He punctuated his next statement with a light kiss. "And we make beautiful love together."

"What about my work?"

"I solemnly promise—" he raised his hand as if taking an oath "—to stay out of your way when you have to work. I'll guard the door to your office. You'll have complete academic seclusion, if that's what you need."

"Seriously, Luke." She voiced her misgivings. "I have a tremendous task before me. My doctoral dissertation. My deadline is less than two months away, and I've got to finish it."

"And so you will. Anything to make the Amber Lady happy." He offered a compromise. "If it doesn't work out, I can always move."

Crystal reviewed the thousand and one reasons

why they should not live together: his work; the campaign; propriety; her therapy sessions. None of them held so much importance as his last flippant comment that he could always move.

Her love for him was too deep for a casual arrangement. If she allowed him to take up residence in her home, there could not be the implied possibility of a separation. "No," she reacted. "My home is not a motel where you can check in and out on a whim. I take my commitments seriously, Luke."

He bit into the last piece of pizza and licked his fingers. His actions contrasted with the gravity of his words. "If my proposition sounded like a casual fling, I apologize. I love you, Crystal. I didn't mean to insult you."

"And I'm not rejecting you." She sought his understanding with wide, pleading eyes. "I care about us, our relationship. Let's give it a chance to grow."

He paced the floor of the bedroom with long impatient strides. The bath towel slipped lower on his hips. He gestured with the remains of the pizza. "There's only one other solution. Will you marry me, Amber Lady?"

She yearned to say "yes," but the strict logic that directed her life reminded her of the looming complications. With completion of her doctorate within a few week's grasp, how could she take on the responsibilities of a wedding and wifehood? There were invitations to order, dresses to buy, family to be notified. Without even beginning to consider the cataclysmic change in her life-style, the thought of marriage made her head spin.

She regarded the tall blond man who stood nearly naked in her bedroom eating pizza. Would she be a good wife for him? Could she fulfill the duties of a political spouse? How should she answer? From her head or from her heart?

His resonant baritone intruded on her thoughts. "You're lovely when you're thinking. You get these two little wrinkles between your eyes and your lips go all quivery." He leered. "And you forget all about the drape of your robe."

She carefully closed the revealing gap of her kimono. "I'm not ready to answer you, Luke. For right now, isn't love enough?"

"More than enough." He released her from the dilemma and sat beside her on the bed. His finger excised the twin worry wrinkles. "For now, I'm happy to love you whenever I can. But I promise you, Amber Lady, that I will ask you again to be my wife. Only once again. And that time, I will expect a definite answer."

10

CRYSTAL SHOVED THROUGH a closetful of wool suits, cotton sundresses and overcoats. Tweed skirts and button-down shirts and a sunny yellow floor-length toga battled for space. She had meant to retire the summer clothing to the cedar closet in the guest bedroom, but her spare time since that hot August night with Luke had been severely limited. Her wardrobe had expanded with the change in weather, and closet organization was low priority on her agenda.

With renewed effort she continued her search for a white silk blouse. While she looked, she haphazardly selected garments to be packed.

She yanked out a blue serge suit of Luke's and threw it on the bed. "He might as well live here," she said aloud as she kicked a pair of black wingtips that squatted incongruously amid her sandals, boots and pumps. "His possessions seem to be accumulating."

Their lives had attained a crazy balance of give-and-take. As Luke's campaign had heated, requiring more of his time, Crystal's work on her dissertation had kept her studying and reading and making midnight trips to her typist with corrections. The practice of kiss therapy had been—in Crystal's opinion—the most unfair intrusion on her time.

Luke was a sought-after public speaker, and before each speech he required Crystal's kiss. To the prying questions of his aides and coworkers, he answered that the kiss was for luck, and most of them had come to accept Crystal as a friendly presence. Only Ms Baumann frowned when Luke wrapped the slender, auburn-haired lady in his strong arms for an embrace before striding to the podium.

Though he tried to compensate for his demand on her time by relieving her of cooking and housekeeping chores, Crystal couldn't help but resent the hours she spent hearing and rehearing the message about Coyote Creek Dam. Weeks ago, she had acknowledged the validity of his arguments, but refused to give him the satisfaction of verbally confirming his stance.

She found the white blouse and pulled it from the clothing on her bed. She wrinkled her nose in disgust. "Honestly, Crystal. You're only spending the weekend in Washington, D.C. Surely, you can be more selective than this."

She tossed aside her long, down coat and then retrieved it. What if there was a cold snap? She went through the same procedure with a lightweight, full-skirted dress and vest. What if it stayed unseasonably warm? She couldn't discard the yellow gown and matching sandals because there just might be a formal dinner party.

Her instinct for being well prepared warred with her need to be efficient. She wasn't a seasoned traveler, and her clothing had never been purchased with the idea of flitting off to unknown climates in unpredictable October weather.

She placed the white blouse against the black wool suit that was definitely correct for several occasions. The conservative colors made it appropriate for business meetings, and the pencil-slim skirt with buttons down the front could be slit to a fashionable height for a chic dinner outfit. That was the ensemble she had chosen to wear on the plane and the only part of her wardrobe that she was sure would be necessary. That and the blue serge suit that Luke had requested in his phone call last night.

He had already been in Washington for three days. Though Crystal had actually looked forward to the brief vacation from Luke's constant attention, she missed him. Her valued privacy and the quiet moments of contemplation that she had once so enjoyed before Luke had stormed into her life seemed hollow and dull. When she had seen him off at the airport, she had assured him that this separation would be good for them. "It will give us a break," she had said. "Maybe we're growing tired of each other. Bored. Complacent."

Three days later, she shook her head emphatically. Bored was not the right answer. His teasing conversation always stimulated her. Events that would have flown by without comment were somehow wonderful when shared. A stroll through the park, a sudden downpour, the Canada geese flying south for the winter—all sparkled with shiny newness. The magical nights of intimacy made a string of perfect pearls that Crystal wore with heightened pride and bright eyes. Boring? Never.

The first night Luke was gone, she soaked in a tangerine scented tub and told herself how much she enjoyed this quiet solitude. The second night, she reread chapter twelve of her dissertation on statistical modes and fell asleep halfway through. By the third night, she had given up her pretense and sat staring at the telephone willing him to call. "Like a silly teenager," she scoffed at herself. Yet, when the phone rang and Luke's voice broke the long-distance static with declarations of love and longing, Crystal's maturity deserted her in a moaning sigh. She missed him terribly and wished she had not been so stubborn in her refusal to accompany him on the whole trip instead of just this Friday and the weekend.

She might not have gone at all except that today Luke was scheduled to address a House subcommittee on water rights for the west. It was the most important speech of his political career, and he couldn't chance a stutter. Crystal had to be there for a kiss of encouragement. She timed her airline reservations to give her a full two hours to make the meeting. "But if I don't get packed, I'll miss the plane."

Almost blindly, she picked her Washington wardrobe and flung the items into two suitcases and a garment bag. There was just enough time for a shower before Ginger came to pick her up.

Crystal had just dressed in the black suit and white silk blouse and lugged her suitcases downstairs when she heard the doorbell. "Are you early?" she asked Ginger.

"Nope. R-r-right on schedule." Her friend eyed the luggage. "This is just a weekend, right? You're not eloping."

"Ginger, you will be the first to know. I promise."

The dark-haired woman tossed aside the flowing serape raincoat that enveloped her and lifted the larger of the bags. "Let's g-g-go. By the way, it's raining."

"So?"

"So, wear a raincoat, ducky. Sometimes I wonder

about your sanity. I mean, you're a great therapist, but sometimes the commonsense department is out to lunch."

"Do I look like I need a lecture?" She grabbed a beige London Fog trench coat from the hall closet. "Hurry. Before I miss my plane."

Crystal settled comfortably into the wide front seat of the red Plymouth station wagon. She cranked the window completely closed against the autumn rain that stirred russet leaves and colored the skies slate gray.

Ginger climbed into the driver's seat and engaged the heavy motor. With a lurch, they merged into traffic. "How's Luke?" she asked.

"Do you realize that since Mr. Todhunter came into my life, you never ask about me? Always Luke. How's Luke? How's the campaign? What's Luke been up to? If I were a jealous woman, I'd question your motives."

"And well you should," Ginger replied vivaciously. "I love you both dearly, but you don't turn me on."

"Does your husband know about this illicit desire?" Crystal asked with raised eyebrows. She had to chuckle as she thought of Charley, a man so laid-back he was practically somnolent. He and Ginger and their two children were the most contented people she had ever known.

"M-m-might do my Charley a bit of good to be jealous," Ginger huffed. "Sometimes I think that old bear takes me for granted."

"I know what you mean," Crystal sympathized, thinking of the weeks of campaigning. "Sometimes I feel like a portable set of lips." She feigned high drama. "Nothing but a sex object."

"Poor baby. Pardon me if I don't feel sorry for you. Every woman in Jefferson County would apply for that job should you decide to retire."

"It's not the sex I'm complaining about," Crystal said with a leer. "It's the doggone inconvenience. Every time he speaks, I have to drop everything and stand by. My schedules are in a shambles. It's amazing that I have any clients left."

"Aren't you exaggerating a teensy bit? M-m-most of Luke's public appearances are in the evening when you're free."

Crystal admitted the truth to her statement, but pointed out that half her workload was academic. Though she had managed to eke out the necessary hours to prepare for and successfully complete her comprehensive exams, she still had the oral defense to work toward. That was the last step on the road to becoming Dr. Crystal Jane Baxter. She coveted every spare moment.

"Listen, honey," Ginger intoned in a wiser-than-thou irony. "I know a way you could save a whole lot of time."

"Tell me," Crystal pleaded. "I'll do anything."

"Get married."

"Almost anything," she quickly amended.

"Why not?" Ginger's emphatic question caused her long, dangling earrings to swing wildly. "If you were married, you could save all this coordination of whereabouts. You would know where he was, and vice versa."

"A marriage of convenience," Crystal mused facetiously. Though Luke had not repeated his proposal, the thought had occurred to her.

"Aha," Ginger pounced. "You're having doubts.

That's a good sign. It shows that maybe for once you're thinking about your own personal happiness, not some esoteric goal you set for yourself when you were twelve."

"I just don't think it's possible to give full concentration to my academic work and plan a wedding at the same time." The excuse sounded feeble. If anything, her relationship with Luke had renewed her enthusiasm for her career. Yet, other doubts continued to nag at the edge of her consciousness. Her role as political appendage was highly unsatisfying, and she often worried about the stutter that had drawn them together. Would Luke love her if he didn't need her therapeutic kiss?

"That excuse won't hold water for long," Ginger reminded. "Your final oral defense is next week, isn't it?"

Crystal's moan confirmed the date.

"Let me plan the wedding," Ginger said cheerfully. "I'd love to play with your combined incomes to design a superlative reception and ceremony."

She outlined the social event of the season—a wedding complete with twelve-tiered cake, African orchids, and Denver's elite in attendance—while Crystal reviewed the obstacles to that occasion.

Ginger screeched to a halt at the passenger drop-off at Stapleton Airport. The area was packed with happy travelers shouting "Bon voyage," expressionless businessmen and crisp stewardesses. Ginger helped Crystal drag her suitcases from the car to the curb and they huddled under the eaves watching the rain. Ginger's hug was a satisfactory farewell. "Have a wonderful trip. And give Luke a special hello for me."

"I *am* telling Charley," Crystal threatened.

"As long as Luke is single," she warned, "he's fair game."

Crystal checked her baggage, hurried to her gate, boarded the plane and sat...and sat...and sat. Outside the porthole, freezing rain fell in relentless sheets. Visibility was practically zero. She checked her new wristwatch, a turquoise and silver bracelet given to her by Luke. When he had buckled it on her wrist, he'd said, "As long as you wear this watch, we have all the time in the world."

She never glanced at that handsome memento without thinking of the tumble into the icy mountain pond when her other watch was irreparably jolted into fast time. "All the time in the world," she said to herself. "Except for right now."

She had only a few scant hours before his scheduled appearance in the House subcommittee. Perhaps, at this very moment, Luke was looking at his own watch, synchronized perfectly with hers, and anticipating her arrival. Perhaps the second hands of both their timepieces swept together round the simple, elegant oval faces. Their heartbeats pounded in secret rhythm half a continent apart.

The pilot's voice came over the airplane's PA system: "Ladies and gentlemen, we have been cleared for takeoff. We regret any inconvenience caused by our delay."

They had been on the ground for an extra half hour, and Crystal suspected that the takeoff might be a slow process given the long line of wide-bodied jets now taxiing toward the runways. What if she was late? What if Luke had to address the subcommittee without benefit of the kiss that released the knot in his throat? Crystal hoped desperately for a tail wind.

Ever since Luke's stuttering debacle in Golden, the possibility of missing connections had haunted her. Somehow, somewhere there might come a time when she was unable to perform kiss therapy. In preparation for that eventuality, she had forced Luke to continue practicing the air-flow technique. She had even tried a substitute operant conditioning where she told him to rub his lips before he approached the podium in the hope that this gesture would remind him of their kisses and thereby alleviate the need for the actual joining of lips. That attempt had been a dismal failure. After Luke had stammered through a few welcoming remarks, he'd excused himself and dashed to Crystal's side. Only her kiss completely dissipated his tongue-tied condition. There was no substitute for the real thing.

She was glad the plane was half-full, and she had no seatmate. Without the need for small talk, she was free to concentrate on urging the plane forward, pitting her will against the forces of nature. They landed an hour and ten minutes late.

With less than an hour to reach the meeting, Crystal raced from the airport and hailed the first taxi. Her tons of luggage would have to be retrieved later.

The cabbie responded to her panic with a bland complacency as they entered the winding complexity of Washington, D.C. This time her progress was impeded by man, not nature. Street repairs slowed traffic to a snail's pace. Crystal clenched and unclenched her fists, vaguely aware that the weather was sunny and bright. The white obelisk of the Washington Monument filled her view, but she had no interest in sightseeing. "Isn't there some other route?" she pleaded.

The cabbie's noncommittal shrug showed her that one route was as slow as another. She rolled down her window and craned her neck into the bumper-to-bumper traffic. The unaccustomed humidity hit her like a sauna, and she began to perspire in her black wool jacket. Clearly the Fates were conspiring against Crystal Baxter as the minutes flew by. Time was running out. Luke needed her, and she was powerless to respond.

Finally, the cab pulled up outside the offices of the House of Representatives beside the Capitol. Crystal darted up the marble stairs and plunged into the labyrinthian depths of the building. Luke had given her the room number, and she impatiently butted to the head of the line at the information desk to ask directions.

Crystal went up one stair, left, then right. Her heels clattered loudly as she ran. She found the room. Her watch showed that she was ten minutes late. Ten minutes. Not much. These committee hearings were notoriously inefficient. It probably hadn't even started yet. She smoothed her auburn hair, lightly frizzed by the damp Washington air, straightened her lapels and entered.

The room was too vast to be considered an office and too small for an auditorium. A long table crossed the front of the room in front of a podium, and four tiers of seats created an arena for the spectators behind a row of desks for the congressmen. As Crystal stumbled through the door no one turned to give her a second glance. A near-capacity crowd hung rapt on every word of the speaker—a tall, lean, blond man whose hair was rumpled boyishly across his forehead.

Luke Todhunter was speaking. His baritone voice held conviction and intelligence. His poise was impressive. He was not stuttering.

Crystal exhaled the breath she had been holding, in a quick gasp. Her heart thudded unbearably in her breast, and she stared across the crowded room.

As he paused for a question from one of the congressmen, Luke met her riveted gaze. He raised his eyebrow and winked, then turned his attention back to the representative from California who had a long, near-filibuster question about watershed and moisture tables.

Only someone who had been watching for that wink would have noticed, and Crystal was grateful to be spared curious scrutiny. She sank into a vacant seat and tried to tame the maelstrom of emotions that brewed within her.

She was proud of her pupil. Luke Todhunter would never be suspected of stuttering. He was exactly in tune with the tenor of the meeting, even comfortable enough to make a wisecrack in response to the congressman who sported a Malibu tan. "You say it never rains in Southern California, it pours?"

The friendly chuckles showed her that Luke was not only making a competent showing, he was winning new and powerful allies. His future in politics was a foregone conclusion. He fairly oozed charisma. His would surely be the new face on the Hill.

Crystal experienced a burning, aching realization. He no longer needed her. He could speak without her kiss. Luke was a free man, and she could almost feel him being drawn away from her in a Washington whirlwind.

She removed her suit jacket, suddenly feeling hot

and sticky in this cloistered atmosphere. A disapproving woman turned and shushed her. Crystal took that simple gesture as a portent of the future. She was out of place, out of order. All these people belonged here. This was their milieu. She had never felt so awkward, like a hayseed from Denver, a bumpkin in these sophisticated halls.

A small rivulet of perspiration trickled between her breasts. She muffled a cough. Her klutziness was unbearable. These people around her—the dark lady with the chic hat, the white-haired gent with razor creases in his trousers, the reporter in a well-tailored suit—*they* never sweated or made gauche gestures. *They* never fled airports without claiming their baggage. The rain never delayed *their* flights, and roads were not repaved in *their* path. Crystal blinked back helpless tears. She would never fit into the life of Luke Todhunter, congressman. And he didn't need her any more, anyway.

She heard the moderator call an end to the afternoon's session, and the scraping of chairs proclaimed the subcommittee hearing to be over. Crystal stood and stretched. The crowd dispersed quickly, and she was alone in the tiered seats. From where she stood, shifting uneasily from foot to foot, she saw well-wishers surrounding Luke.

He detached himself and bounded up the stairs to her side, all smiles and ebullience. "You look like a breath of clean fresh air, my Amber Lady. I was afraid you'd never arrive."

"Fresh air?" she said with a breeziness she didn't feel. "And here I thought I was practically dripping with chic."

"Like all these other cold fish," he whispered with

a shudder, his warm breath tickling her ear. "That severe suit only makes you look more vibrant and alive."

She avoided his deep blue eyes. Apparently, he didn't yet see how her brand of vibrancy marked her as peculiar among these Washington sophisticates.

"Is something the matter?" he asked with genuine concern. "Why were you so late?"

"Colorado rain and Washington street repairs." She covered her unhappiness with small talk, hoping to elude his questions. "If you could have seen the downpour I just left, you would never again worry about the Colorado watershed. People were building arks and planning to evacuate the zoo two by two."

He chuckled appreciatively. "I've missed you, Crystal. Nobody here ever laughs."

Before she could reply, a reporter overtook Luke. His oddly phrased inquiries were designed to showcase his own expertise on the subject of water rights. Though the other politicians had fled the room, Luke patiently attempted to answer the reporter's questions with honest deliberation.

After ten minutes of holding a frozen smile, Crystal felt her discomfort vanish when the reporter asked her identity. She wondered how he would respond: this is Crystal—I summoned her as an example of the small-town folks in Denver; or, she's my current love interest, a bit of humanity for your column; or, this is my own special, political appendage.

He surprised her. "This is Crystal Baxter, a highly respected speech language pathologist from Denver."

"And what is she doing in Washington?"

The third-person phrasing of the question made Crystal feel totally invisible. She put her foot down with a resounding thud. "I am here in a professional capacity to advise Mr. Todhunter on his speaking manner."

"Anything else?" came the sly innuendo.

"Not a single thing that concerns you." Her blunt discourtesy contrasted with Luke's easy charm, but Crystal could not have cared less. She was not running for office and would be damned if she would become the topic for some well-dressed reporter's gossip. "Shall we go, Mr. Todhunter?"

With a shrug and a grin, Luke escorted her through the halls of the Congressional Office Building. Several individuals offered casual greetings. Others shook Luke's hand and congratulated him on his successful appearance before the subcommittee. It was apparent to Crystal that Luke had made a good impression on the staid folks of government. They wanted to touch him, to bask in his reflected glory, to be remembered. Yet, he seemed oblivious to their conniving intent.

Crystal grew exasperated with their slow progress down the long corridor. Under her breath, she snapped a catty comment, "I've never seen so many tongues hanging out. They all want to ride on your coattails."

"Why? I'm a nobody from out west."

"Please spare me the false modesty, Todhunter," she said with clipped tones. "You are the hero of the hour. Must be the season for idealistic environmentalists."

They paused to exchange quick repartee with someone Crystal recognized from the six o'clock news, and she confirmed her jaded cynicism. "See? That old bigot doesn't give one hoot about your water rights and Coyote Creek Dam. He's meeting you as a colleague, a very photogenic newcomer to the scene.

Everybody wants to crawl into bed with you, make lasting connections, give favors you will have to reciprocate when elected.''

''There's only one person I intend to crawl into bed with,'' he said softly. His hand pressed into the small of her back to guide her, and Crystal felt the old familiar chemistry that jingled her nerves and made her legs feel like rubber. ''I've missed you, Crystal.''

She wished she could return his warmth and tell him how much she'd yearned for him during this brief three-day separation, but the words caught in her throat. She saw the graffiti on the wall, and it told her Luke was destined to leave her. He was captivated, willingly or not, by the power of government. Excitement fairly sparked from him, and there was no niche for Crystal in his brilliant future.

Perversely, she found herself hoping for his failure. If only he had stuttered at the meeting, he might be condemned to remain at her level. His success was frightening because it broke the therapeutic bond that tied them together. He didn't need her.

She reminded herself that dwelling on tragedy was not her style. She required a course of action, and the only route that stood before her was to gracefully withdraw her companionship. She ought to be glad for him and to willingly step aside. At least his mother would be happy.

''Congratulations, Luke,'' she said, suppressing her bitterness. ''You spoke very well today. In my professional opinion, you've got your dysfluency under control.''

''I was scared,'' he confided. ''When I saw I was going to have to speak without you, I almost cancelled.''

''What stopped you?''

"Bald pride and fantasy. I wouldn't give up without a fight. And I did that lip-rubbing, kiss-remembering exercise. I guess we've stored up enough to get me through a few situations." Unmindful of the watching eyes in the corridor, he nuzzled her cheek. "Let's make sure I never run short."

She pulled free and phrased a suspicious question. "Is this the first time you've spoken to a group without me?"

"Of course. Why?" Confusion reflected in his chiseled features. "You don't think I've been stringing you along?"

"Maybe. You were awfully smooth at that podium." Power rode easily on his broad shoulders, she thought. He was clever enough to manipulate, while maintaining an engaging, naive idealism. "Washington seems to agree with you."

"I'm a tourist here, Crystal. Just like you." He shook off the coldness that was growing between them. "So why don't we act like a couple of visitors from Colorado. Let's go to the National Air and Space Museum and see the Apollo II module."

She rolled back her eyes. He was treating her like a child.

"What do you say, Amber Lady? May I fly you to the moon?"

They strolled side by side into the warm sunlight, but Crystal shivered. She feared the stormy weather that lay ahead.

11

Luke reached out tentatively and touched the moon rock on display at the front entrance of the National Air and Space Museum. The surface was rough and homely, not at all like an exotic specimen.

He glanced at the auburn-haired woman, named Crystal after another semiprecious mineral. "What would your father, the geologist, say about that rock that traveled 240,000 miles?"

Her shoulders rose and fell with a noticeable lack of excitement, a gesture that was significant in its disdain. But Luke refused to let his high spirits be dampened. He imagined that she was exhausted from her frustrating trip and made it his business to cheer her up. "I guess he'd comment on the fact that it's not an impressive hunk of stone. Maybe he'd say that not every miracle is beautiful. Sometimes, the best finds are right in your own backyard."

She simply sighed, strolled a few paces and fixed her eyes on the Wright brothers' first flying machine.

Her back view pleased him. Even in this grumpy mood, she held her head erect and proud. The crisp undulation of her walk always made him think of a woman with purpose, and the slim, black skirt gracefully outlined the curve of her cute little bottom. Why was she so edgy while he was sky high?

It's just a mood, he thought. *She'll shake it off.* Luke

had discovered a great deal during their three-day separation. His depth of feeling for Crystal and their relationship was the most important and obvious revelation. Just thinking that she was fifteen hundred miles away—as far as the moon for all intents and purposes—had caused him sleepless nights and an adolescent, lovesick loss of appetite. He knew he had to marry this woman quickly so they need never by apart again.

On another level, he'd learned that his political career would be a short-lived venture. Certain data showed that federal funding would not be allocated for the Coyote Creek Dam project. Without the funds from Washington, the state of Colorado would never undertake such an extremely costly endeavor. The dam had been stopped. Luke had won his battle by default. There was no longer a reason for this one-issue candidate to continue his pursuit of congressional office.

It was a deep, abiding relief to him that he would not have to leave Colorado. This short stay in Washington had also shown him that the mountains were his home, the place he belonged and loved. He never wanted to leave for something as silly to him as politics.

Crystal stopped beside the command module from Apollo II. He joined her and took her hand. "Do you remember the first moon walk?" he asked with unflagging cheerfulness. "A giant step for mankind? Small step for a man?"

"I didn't believe it was real," she said glumly. "It seemed like a fuzzy replay from one of those awful Japanese science-fiction movies."

"What a cynic."

"I kept expecting some giant cucumber to slither over the horizon and gobble up Neil Armstrong."

Luke recalled his lecture to himself just after hanging Crystal's wallpaper. Sitting at her kitchen table, he confronted his unwillingness to trust. "You have to believe in something," he said meaningfully. "The Apollo mission. The unchanging stars and tide. Other people."

He saw a shadow cross her gold-flecked eyes. Ever since her arrival in Washington, she had been so strange and distant. He had offered laughter and love, but she pushed it away with both hands. What a lousy political wife she would be! With all her moods transparent in her expressive face, he was glad he did not truly aspire in that direction. "Still thinking about your luggage?"

"Well, it was so incredibly dumb. I have enough clothes to change every fifteen minutes, and here I am wearing wool during a heat wave."

"You look great, very neat and appropriate."

"With a raincoat tucked under my arm?" Her voice was uncharacteristically flat and complaining. "In my suitcase, which is probably lost at the airport, I have a nifty little sundress with bare shoulders and a short-sleeved jacket."

"As much as I'd like to see your naked shoulders, I prefer the suit. You're not meant to be a decorative woman."

He winced as he realized that his comment could easily be misinterpreted. His intention had been to praise her, to tell her that she was more than a pretty face, that she was a woman of substance. Her grimace told him that she had taken it wrong. "What I mean, Crystal, is that you are head and shoulders—naked or not—above most of the feather-headed, designer-packaged ladies who inhabit this town."

"I suppose you've taken a survey." She tugged at one springy curl and pouted, "I don't think this climate agrees with me. The humidity is doing wonders for my naturally frizzy hair."

She strode toward the stairs leading to an upper mezzanine, and again he puzzled at her mood. Perhaps, he worried, the separation that had convinced him of his love had affected her differently. Maybe she had found his absence to her liking. The thought sliced through him like a bolt of lightning. Maybe she'd rethought their relationship and wanted to end it. He had to penetrate the bitterness behind her tawny eyes. "What's wrong, Crystal?"

"Look at that." She paused before an old monoplane. *The Spirit of St. Louis.*"

Luke's attention transferred from her to the old plane. Despite his anxiety, the flimsy aircraft filled him with awe. Its small rickety body had supported the first solo flight from New York to Paris. As Luke now launched his own shaky effort, he was inspired by the brave determination of its pilot. "Charles Lindbergh. Now there was a real hero."

"More impressive than the astronauts?"

"Different. He was a pioneer. A lone man conquering the unknown. He didn't have radio contact with Houston. Just a couple of Hershey bars and tremendous willpower."

"The first man to solo the Atlantic," she mused. "A bit like your own solo flight this afternoon when you addressed the subcommittee all by yourself."

"You can't compare the two. My speech was like a milk run when stacked up beside Lindbergh's flight."

"I don't know. It took a sort of heroism."

The two parallel worry wrinkles appeared between her eyes. One corner of her lips pulled downward in an expression of concern that Luke had come to recognize as symptomatic of inner tension. "Does my solo flight bother you?" he asked gently. "Would you rather have had me crash and burn."

"Of course not. I couldn't be more delighted." Her rapid change of subject as she pointed to another exhibit told him that he was on the right trail.

"You'll never make a politician, Crystal. You're no good at being evasive," he accused. "You're angry because I was able to speak without you."

"Don't be idiotic. I'm a therapist, remember? My whole professional purpose is to see my clients cured."

"Look at me, Crystal. What do you see? Another client?" He followed her to the edge of the balcony. "Do you want me to fail?" he asked.

Her lip quivered slightly. The deep sadness of downcast eyes warred with her proud spirit. She swallowed hard and banished her tears. "I want you to be happy," she said. "Whatever it takes."

"Happy? You can do better than that, Crystal." His patience snapped at the realization of her vulnerable misery. Why couldn't she tell him what was wrong? He grasped her arm roughly and turned her to face him. "You're a professional communicator. You should be able to tell me what's wrong instead of acting like a witch."

"You once said I was your lovely amber witch. You liked me that way."

"I was talking about an enchantress, not a hag. And don't change the subject. Does it bother you that I didn't stutter?"

"Yes," she shouted. She met his ice-blue eyes with her fire-filled gaze. "Your easy diplomacy infuriates me. I hate to see the way you've adapted so neatly to this two-faced city. I hate the way you've used me."

Luke dropped her arm. His hand felt cold and numb where he'd touched her. He had been blinded by his hopes and dreams—blind to her true character. She was just like any other woman. She pitied him, cared for him as a handicapped fool to be mothered and petted. A wrenching tightness convulsed deep in his belly.

He verbally turned the knife in their writhing, dying relationship. "Can't you love a whole man? Would you rather spend your life with a cripple?"

"What are you talking about?"

"The stutter." He spat the words. "You loved me for my stutter. You don't like the idea that I might be an independent human being."

He ignored her protest and continued, unable to stem the hurtful tide. At least, this was a situation with which he was familiar. How many times had he chosen to reject before being rejected?

"I thought you were different," he said. "I thought you might understand that there is more to me than a stammer, that our relationship could be based on something more than the fact that I can't speak without making a fool of myself. But I was wrong. You don't want me unless I am safely under your thumb."

"Oh, how clever and bright you are. How perceptive." She clenched the railing of the balcony. "Surely you've noticed how very much I have *not* enjoyed trailing after you at all your public appearances. Only a complete imbecile, Todhunter, could miss how nicely I have *not* fitted into the role of political supporter."

"I never forced you."

"You did. You used your stutter like a ball and chain. It's your guilt, Todhunter, not mine."

He lost track of her reasoning. Why was she babbling about politics? That part of his life was over. "Exactly what are you accusing me of? What have I done?"

"You haven't been honest. You're building a future, a bright future that doesn't include me. I would respect you more if you would just tell me—straight forward and direct—that you want to get rid of me."

"Get rid of you?"

"That's what this is all about, isn't it? Big deal politician makes good. Leaves lover. That's the whole problem in a nutshell. You don't n-n-need me anymore."

He was immobilized by a confused rush of emotions. She thought he was rejecting her. And he was, but not because of some political goal. He was pushing her away because he loved her and could not stand her pity. What had happened to them? What vindictive fate had twisted his love. His throat was paralyzed. He was unable to speak or even move.

"I'm leaving, Luke. I have to sort things out. Nothing's making sense."

He watched her descend the stairs without looking back. She crossed the lobby, passed the space module and the Wright brothers' plane and strode into the gathering Washington dusk.

FRESH AIR FANNED THE HOTNESS of her cheek. A wide sidewalk stretched before her, and she concentrated on placing one foot before the other, desiring nothing more than a wide distance between herself and the scene of her debasement. "At least I had the courage to leave," she muttered. "At least I avoided a messy scene."

She scanned the blank facades of ornate white buildings bordering the mall. Where was she going? Did it matter? She hated herself with a depth of passion that equaled the feeling she had formerly identified as love. Why couldn't she be what he wanted?

She joined the anonymous herd of bureaucrats leaving their offices. It was well past departure time for the nine-to-five shift, but the streets were still filled with late workers who'd put in that extra twenty minutes to get ahead. They were going home, but where was home for Crystal Baxter?

Her Victorian house in Denver? It was so far away and so completely suffused with the presence of Luke. How could she think of him leaving? It would be a huge job to reclaim her privacy. His clothing would have to be packed and shipped to his condominium. His books would have to be crated. His toothbrush burned. She would have to paint over the wallpaper that he had helped to hang. There were so many untidy little things.

She filled her mind with details, not daring to dwell on the larger picture. A life without Luke would be so hollow and dull. She forced the thought from her mind. Rorschach the cat would never forgive her. Marv at the deli would be distraught.

The Washington Monument loomed before her, a shaft of white masonry that pierced the sunless skies as surely as the arrow that stabbed her heart. The purity of the obelisk rebuked her. In its shadow, the government performed its three-ring circus of influence in arenas that were utterly foreign to her thinking.

She imagined the future congressman from Colorado—Luke Todhunter with his sun-streaked hair and healthy tan—standing beside the monument. His righteous idealism matched its clean, soaring lines. Would he ever think of her?

Despite her brave resolutions, tears welled up in her eyes. Would he miss her if she called an end to their love? Her future lay before her like a long corridor of closed doors. Only Luke held the keys, and she was unable to open them without his help. Behind one of the doors, she imagined the peal of their laughter. Behind another, their lovemaking sounded in cries of passion that Crystal knew would never be equaled in her lifetime. She had found the one great love of her life.

"I don't want to be alone again," she said to herself. "But I can't be a politician's wife. Where do I go from here?"

She concentrated on the sure future. Her professional accomplishments should provide some comfort. In five days, she would present her oral defense of her dissertation. Barring catastrophe, she would be awarded her doctoral degree. Yet, the pride she should have felt tasted stale. That diploma would never keep her warm at night.

Another presence paused to stare at the monument, and Crystal self-consciously wiped her unshed tears. A familiar baritone voice spoke from the gathering gloom. "Crystal. I love you. You can't deny love. It exists. Almost has a life of its own. I love you."

Her heart leaped, but she forced herself to stare straight ahead at the monument, not trusting herself to face him. "I can't be the woman you need. You have to have someone who will be comfortable with all this. Somebody who glitters. I'll never be an effective, political spouse."

He stepped into her line of vision and lifted her chin. His intense gaze stabbed through her, unleashing all the longing she was trying to suppress. "Who says I need a political wife?"

"You d-do." The powerful chemistry between them threw her off balance. She felt her reined emotions straining to be free. "You're g-g-going to b-be a c-c-congressman."

"I want you. I want to see your smile." He tangled his fingers in the luxuriant waves of her auburn hair. "My lovely Amber Lady, you are the only woman I will ever want or need."

"You still don't understand." As her explanation forced them apart, her body clove nearer to him. She was drawn by the warm vortex of their shared tenderness. "I don't fit into your future. I cannot follow you to Washington."

"I'm not going to Washington. I'll never leave the mountains. They are as much a part of me as you."

"But the dam? Your career? What about that?" She stemmed a rising tide of hope. "You're not dropping out of the campaign, are you?"

"I found out today that the federal government has no intention of funding Coyote Creek Dam. Without that fiscal support, the dam is a dead issue. Colorado can't afford it."

"But what about all the other legislation? The schools? Mass transportation?"

"I'll leave those causes to some other idealist. I was a one-issue candidate, and as far as I'm concerned the fight is over. I've won."

Crystal was still suspicious. "You could win the

whole election, Luke. I've seen how you took this
jaded city by storm. Heroes don't usually stop mid-
stream."

"Lindbergh did. He flew the Atlantic and then re-
tired from the limelight." He cracked a smile that
seemed free and guileless, and Crystal recognized his
sincerity. "Tell me, Therapist Lady, what have I always said I wanted to do with my life? Have you been
listening?"

"You want to be a trial lawyer," she repeated by
rote. "One of those nutty public defenders who take
on lost causes."

"And why have I not pursued this career?"

"The stutter."

"And what happened today?"

"You don't have to treat me like some half-wit. I can
see where you are leading."

"Now, let's see if you can catch a curve ball," he
said, teasingly. His finger traced her jawline and
crossed her lips in an old-fashioned gesture for silence. "I don't expect you to be a political wife. I don't
want you to stand in the background with my slippers and pipe. I want to share with a woman who has
her own interests, her own career, her own sphere of
growth."

A tide of ecstasy was building within her, surging
to uncontrollable proportions. She wasn't the ideal
woman, but his description fit her very nicely. How
could she have doubted? He was everything she
wanted in a man. Why shouldn't the jigsaw pieces
match for him? She spoke past his silencing finger.
"May I say something?"

"Speak."

"Does it matter if this woman has frizzy hair?"

"Has to have frizzy hair." He cradled her head and pulled her toward him, easily molding her pliant softness to his masculine strength. When his lips covered her mouth, Crystal felt the tidal wave of desire crashing all around her.

Their kiss was fierce, filled with powerful longing. They twined on the shadowless hill before the Washington Monument. Their doubts and fears dissolved in lovers' bliss. Crystal escaped the dismal future that she'd conjured only moments before and ran free through the corridors of her heart. All the doors swung wide, and all her tomorrows beckoned brightly.

She wriggled in his arms, feeling the undeniable masculine evidence of his desire for her. Gazing up at the pure white obelisk, she said, "It never struck me before, but don't you think the monument is a trifle obscene?"

He nodded in mock seriousness. "No wonder they have so many sex scandals in Washington." He took her hand and led her to Constitution Avenue. "You know, I've heard that there's a niche behind the Lincoln Memorial that's just big enough for two people."

"Kinky. But I prefer a king-sized bed." Her delicate eyebrow arched questioningly. "How did you happen to be chatting about niches? And with whom?"

"Gosh, Crystal." His eyes widened innocently. "It's hard telling. There have been so-o-o-o many."

"Well, then. I guess I have my work cut out for me. I've got to erase all those sophisticated cats." She reached up and grabbed his ear. "Let's go, Todhunter. How far to the Lincoln Memorial?"

"Our hotel is closer."

Though gossamer wings eluded the Colorado lovers, Luke did manage to hail a cab. In moments they were transported to Washington's most elegant hotel. Chandeliers and liveried bellboys and carpet of ankle-deep plushness passed before them in a haze. Their magnificent surroundings went unnoticed as they sailed through in a misty awareness of nothing but the longing of their two bodies.

Crystal followed him into his suite and watched as he closed and locked the ornate white-and-gold painted door. She was alone with him, and nothing else existed. A sense of triumph curled her lips. Luke Todhunter, the handsome, idealistic, former politician was hers alone. She felt like an early prospector who had just discovered the mother lode.

He crossed the room in wide strides as graceful as a stalking panther finding his willing prey. "I love your smile, Amber Lady. What are you thinking about?"

"Since my luggage is still at the airport, I don't have a thing to wear to bed."

"Since when has that been a problem?"

"For special occasions—like weekends in glamorous hotels—I keep a few seductive nighties." She removed her black jacket and draped it across a Louis Quinze settee. "I packed two."

"Why haven't I ever seen these seductive peignoirs?" He undid his tie and tossed the scrap of patterned silk atop her jacket. His suit coat followed. "I've never noticed them in your closet."

She dawdled with the pearl buttons on her shirt-front. "They were in my hope chest."

His lips twitched with suppressed laughter as he unbuttoned his cuffs. "I thought that tradition went out with dowries."

The white silk shirt slithered from her shoulders.

This game of seductive undressing while conducting a normal conversation titillated her. She pretended not to notice the virile expanse of his chest as he unbuttoned his own shirt. She continued her chatter. "The cedar chest at the foot of my bed is full of hand-embroidered pillowcases and nighties and a painted china teapot." She kicked off her shoes and wiggled out of her panty hose. "I've had very high hopes, Luke."

He peeled off his shirt. "Have any of your fantasies been fulfilled?"

Crystal slid her pencil-slim skirt down her legs, and stood before him in silken underclothing trimmed with white lace. "Almost all of them."

He ran his finger round the lace edge of her panties. "What's left?"

"Maybe we'll find out tonight." She gasped at the smooth caress of his powerful hand, slipped from his grasp and pranced to the bedroom door. "I'll be waiting in here, Todhunter."

Luke sat down to remove his shoes and socks, a simple act that was fraught with eroticism to her heightened senses.

"I'm so glad you did that," she said from the bedroom door. "Men with black socks on bare legs are funny-looking. Always make me think of my father mowing the lawn in his Bermuda shorts and wing-tips."

"Now I know you're completely recovered," Luke said. "You're going to favor me with another of Papa Baxter's quotes, aren't you?"

"'When the leaves turn green, it doesn't always mean that spring is here. Be ready for June blizzards.'"

"Spoken like a true Coloradoan," he commended. "But what does it mean?"

She tossed him a seductive leer and disappeared into the bedroom. "I'll tell you when I have you where I want you." In case he missed her point, she added, "In here."

Crystal barely had time to strip off her bra and panties and slide between the sheets before Luke appeared in the doorway. He had also discarded his clothing. "Tell me," he said, as he leaned indolently against the door frame.

"Even when things are going well, there's always the possibility of a misunderstanding." She shuddered. "Like what happened between us today."

Instantly, he was at her side offering comfort and succor. He gathered her into his arms and held her close, his body protecting her from the painful memories. She luxuriated in the warm contact of flesh against flesh. "I never stopped loving you," she quietly explained. "When I saw you speaking before that committee, all I could think was you didn't need me anymore."

She shivered as his fingers lightly stroked the delicate line of her vertebrae. His voice was husky. "I'll always need you."

The patterns of their lovemaking had changed constantly in the time from August to October. Each had learned the secrets of the other's body and could choose the texture of arousal.

Luke knew of her sensitive inner thigh. He had found the nerve endings at the base of her spine.

She had discovered an urgent eroticism in pectoral massage and attention to his ear.

They used these and other sensual manipulations

to choreograph their passion. Their dance of love was amazingly tender and sensitive as their bodies sought to heal their earlier misunderstandings.

As they scaled the heights of ecstasy in throbbing union, he rolled to his side. Still joined with her, he continued the rhythmic pressure. On his back, he lifted her above him and guided her hips astride his body. He fondled the swell of her small breasts and the womanly curve of her waist.

Looking down on his firm, muscular torso, Crystal experienced a sensation of power. Her motion controlled the ebb and flow, moving from excruciating slowness to a hard-driving culmination.

The cooled air of the elegant hotel room swirled against her moist skin as she realized the moment when neither could give another degree. She collapsed on his chest and expelled a long, fulfilled sigh.

Together, they flew to the enchanted world beyond the realm of human understanding. Her limbs felt feather light as she rolled from him and nestled at his side.

"I love you, Luke." The simple declaration seemed insufficient for the torrents he unleashed in her. "Do you think we're better after we've argued?"

"No comment. I don't want you to be encouraged to pick fights." He brushed her cheek with a tender, butterfly kiss. "We're always terrific."

"Definitely a ten," she said with a contented smile.

"You can't grade miracles, my lovely Amber Lady." He smoothed the wild tangle of her hair. "I have a surprise for you."

"Sorry, love. I can't take any more."

"One-track mind." He left her side and went to the closet where two other suits were neatly hung. When he returned, his hands were hidden behind his back. "Guess which hand."

"Don't I get to pick what's behind Door Number Three?" She propped herself up on one elbow. "All right. I pick the left."

"And the little lady wins the prize." He presented her with a small velvet-covered box.

She lifted the lid on its hinges to reveal a delicately wrought band of gold. Centered in its intricate tracery was a pear-shaped diamond that sent prisms of reflected light dancing through the room. "It's beautiful," was all she could say.

"I know what you're thinking," he said softly. "It looks like an engagement ring. It feels like an engagement ring. If it had odor, it would probably smell like an engagement ring. But I'm not trying to force you into any commitment."

She raised dubious eyes to meet his. "If it's not an engagement ring, what is it?"

"A gift."

Despite a flurry of conflicting emotions, Crystal couldn't help touching the ring. The gold beckoned her to slide the band onto the third finger of her left hand. Nothing would give her more satisfaction than to accept.

She willed herself to hesitate. Her oral examination for her doctorate was scheduled for the following week. She'd stayed clear of commitments thus far. Right now, single-minded concentration on her goal was vitally important. She placed the ring back into its box and closed the lid. "Give me one more week."

"It's only a gift," he protested. "I know how important this week is to you. I only wanted to give you something. To make a link between us."

"A link is part of a chain, and I can't believe that this beautiful ring is nothing more than a token of your affection."

"You're right," he admitted quietly. "It is meant to be an engagement ring."

The portent of his words hung heavily in the air. He had vowed to ask her only once again, and she was unready to answer. "Just one more week," she pleaded.

"Dammit, Crystal. I'm not asking you to give anything up. This ring will signify nothing more than a future. I don't expect you to stop studying and iron my shirts because I've given you a ring."

Her fears and doubts resurfaced and washed through her mind, erasing logic. "How can I explain when my brain is full of dissertation. I'm nervous, Luke. I don't want to come to you like this. You deserve a complete woman. It's such a total lifetime commitment, and I don't have time—"

He exploded. "When do you think you can make the time, Crystal? Next week or next year? Your professional commitments aren't going to stop with the dissertation."

He stormed across the plush bedroom in wide strides, went into the outer room and closed the door behind him.

Crystal reclined on the sheets. Their cool, smooth texture could not soothe her fevered anxiety. Unconsciously, she rubbed the velvet box still clutched in her hand. Only moments before, she had floated at the apex of ecstasy, and now she had plummeted to despair.

She couldn't just lie there and accept her fate. The future—their future together—hung by a tenuous thread. If she allowed him to leave, that thread would snap, and the fabric of their love would never be mended.

Frantically, she wrapped the sheet around her like a toga and stumbled to the door. "Don't leave me, Luke."

"Save it." He thrust his arms into his wrinkled shirt. "You need all your energy for the day of your orals."

"Forgive me." Her voice cracked. "I'll do anything you ask, just don't leave me."

Her awkward robe made a long, tangled trail behind her. She took two wobbly steps toward him and extended one hand in mute appeal.

The coldness in his eyes melted as he came slowly toward her. His hand raised and found hers. Their fingers meshed. "My darling," he whispered. "What are we doing to each other?"

He gathered her into a fierce embrace. "I'm sorry, so sorry." She felt a tremor run through him. "I never meant to upset you."

"It's me," she said as she clung breathlessly to him. "Half the time I don't know what I'm doing. I'm crazy with nerves."

The truth of her unpredictable behavior crept over the edge of her subconscious mind into recognized reality. The pressure of her impending academic trial had thrown her usually sensible manner into chaos. That anger and fear quaked through her and threatened her future with Luke.

She was ashamed of her weakness and vowed to control the inner volcano. She forced herself to stand firm and straight, but still nestled against his chest. "I should be apologizing to you, Luke. My behavior has been reprehensible. What can I do to make amends?''

"First, you can stop talking to me like you're taking a vocabulary test."

A healing smile broke across her face. "I only do that—"

"When you're upset. I know." He paused thoughtfully. "Second, you can believe me when I say that I will never leave you. As long as you'll have me, I'll be here for you."

"Is there a third?"

"Never two without three." He stroked her back in a comforting gesture. "What happened between us is my fault. It was stupid and selfish to make you come to Washington this weekend."

"I wanted to come," she objected. "I missed you terribly."

"No," he gently corrected. "You were right when you said that I was using my stutter like a ball and chain. I forced you to come to my rescue when you should be home resting up for your exam."

His light, lambent touch claimed her furrowed brow. "I'm going to give you an ultimatum, Crystal. We leave Washington first thing in the morning and get you back where you belong."

"We don't have to cut short our vacation, Luke."

"Somehow, I don't think we'll be able to do much relaxing in each other's company. There's too much crowding in on us." His jaw tightened. "Remember, I'm going to disappoint a lot of people in Denver. My loyal friends believed in me and supported my candidacy. It won't be easy to tell them the party's over."

Crystal felt a hot, embarrassed flush rising from her

neck. Her total self-absorption had kept her from con-
sidering the problems confronting Luke. She imagined
the stricken look on Ms Baumann's face, the tears of his
political groupies and the righteous arguments. His situation equaled hers in stress.

"I've asked you to marry me, Crystal. But I don't
want your answer. Not yet. First, you have to complete your goal. I say we put our relationship on hold
until you are Dr. Baxter. Five more days."

She had to admit there was a good deal of common
sense in that arrangement. At least, they wouldn't be
sniping at each other, taking out their other antago-
nisms in hurtful arguments. "I'll still see you, won't
I?"

"I'm not going to disappear. I'll just stay quietly in
the background. No pushing for the next five days."

"Then what?"

"We take up where we left off."

"I don't know." She snuggled up to him. "I might
miss the old, irascible, passionately idealistic Luke."

"It's only until Wednesday." He drew a smile on
her lips. "Besides, we still have tonight."

12

CRYSTAL SPENT the days before her oral defense reviewing every page of every textbook on Speech Pathology. She was intellectually primed, but depleted in all other ways. Her hair went uncombed. Sleep was impossible. The very thought of food made her break out in a cold sweat. She misplaced coffee cups, note pads, shampoo and twenty-dollar bills.

Rorschach would have starved if Luke had not dropped by every evening to prepare Crystal's dinner, meals that usually went uneaten. He always left after cleaning up the dishes. Their conversations were purposely indifferent.

"How's the studying?" he would carefully ask.

"Awful. There's so much heavy data crammed in my head that my hair should go straight."

"I know you can do it, kid. I believe in you."

Though he steadfastly offered encouragement, he never went beyond performing the simple tasks of daily existence that she had come to neglect. He treated her like an invalid, catering to her whims, seeing to her needs and avoiding meaningful contact.

Once she demanded, "I want you to stay the night."

He parried with a convenient excuse. "I have a meeting."

"Afterward?"

He patted her hand. "You need your sleep. For that matter, so do I."

She dropped the subject, unable to summon the necessary energy to insist. On a reasonable level, she knew his schedule was exhausting. The newspapers were filled with Luke Todhunter's unexpected withdrawal from his campaign. He used the forum to throw his support behind another idealistic statesman and spoke unceasingly on that man's behalf. She knew his work load was incredible and was surprised that he found time to be so solicitous.

On the morning of her oral defense, Crystal dressed with special care. She covered the signs of her nervousness with artistic makeup. A red wool blazer and plaid pleated skirt disguised her thinness. She conditioned her auburn hair to a glistening shine and piled it atop her head. With two hours until the final, she was ready. There was ample time to pace and fret.

The telephone rang, and she answered, "Hello, handsome."

"Handsome yourself. This is Ginger. J-j-just called to wish you luck."

"Thanks." Crystal paused. "Well? Aren't you going to ask me about Luke?"

"Today—and just for today, mind you—I am only c-c-concerned with you."

Crystal soundlessly snapped her fingers. "No p-p-p-problem." She gasped.

"What's the matter, dear?"

"D-d-didn't you hear me?"

"I believe it's called a stutter, Crystal." Ginger took the part of therapist. "Quite normal under the circumstances. Take a d-d-deep breath and try again."

"Okay." Crystal regained her control. "There. It's gone. Wouldn't that be a nightmare? Going for an oral test in Speech Pathology and stuttering?" Her attempt at laughter was painfully stiff.

"Do you need a ride to the university?" Ginger masked her deep uneasiness with a light tone. "Oh, but that's silly of me. I'm sure Luke is right there holding your hand."

"He has a press conference at two, the same time as my oral, but he's going to meet me afterward. Don't worry, Ginger. I'm fine."

"Are you eating lunch? You'd better be eating lunch."

"Of course," Crystal lied. "I'm all dressed and ready to go."

She said goodbye and sat staring at the phone, almost catatonic. The tiny slip in her speech fluency had had a devastating effect, and she fervently wished for Luke's comforting presence. Last night he had offered to cancel his speaking engagement to come with her, and she had blithely assured him that she was absolutely in control.

She now cursed that phony self-confidence. Why couldn't she have admitted that she needed him? She held one small hand before her and watched it tremble like an aspen leaf. *All I need is a nice cup of tea*, she told herself. *Or a fifth of whiskey. Or twelve Valium.*

She puttered in the kitchen and paced in the hall and finally went to her bedroom. In her top dresser drawer, she found the black velvet box. Within it lay the diamond ring Luke had given her, symbolic of the loving chain that would bind her to him. Purposefully, she slid the ring onto her third finger, left hand. The time for commitment was near enough, and the delicate gold tracery was a comforting reminder of Luke's support.

On the drive to the university, Crystal entertained the most ridiculous fantasies. *What if I have an accident? What if there's an earthquake and my car is swallowed up? Is it the right day? The right time?*

She knew her most severe questioner would be Dr. Leona Freeman. That steely-eyed lady had questioned Crystal's thesis from the start and had objected several times to another paper on stuttering even though Crystal's approach was fresh and untested. Crystal hoped she was thoroughly versed in all possible refutations of her arguments.

She entered the building in a daze, barely nodding to the secretary who wished her a cheery "good luck." Other students passed by her in silence, understanding the jitters that had claimed one of their number. They paused to offer a smile or a handshake. A cup of coffee appeared beside her, and Crystal drank without thinking.

She watched the professorial members of her committee file into the conference room. Her advisor, Dr. John MacConnell, placed his hand on her shoulder and said, "Try to relax, Crystal. You have nothing to worry about. Your thesis—as I've told you countless times—is excellent."

"Yes sir, I mean, no sir. I mean yes sir, I do have something to worry about, but...thank you, sir."

Why was she babbling like an idiot? Waving her arms in silly gestures? She carefully folded one hand on top of the other and closed her mouth. Her oral defense of her dissertation represented the culmination of her academic career, the most important event in her life. Why was she acting like a fool? Her shoulders slumped beneath Dr. MacConnell's hand. Her poor eating habits and insomnia had drained her completely.

Dr. MacConnell noted the pale face before him. "Are you feeling unwell? Should I request a postponement?"

"Oh no, sir." The thought of postponement was agonizing. Crystal doubted her physical ability to go through this preparation again. It was now or never. "I'll be fine. Really, I will."

The professor's kindly brown eyes assessed her. "You look exhausted, Crystal. What' bothering you?"

"Just nerves. Jitters."

She paused. Her fingers unconsciously twisted the golden ring and she realized that something was bothering her—Luke's absence. She had been there for him, offering support and understanding every time he needed her. Where was he? "It's only nervousness," she lied.

"If your dissertation were not so thorough, and I did not believe that you were a shoo-in candidate, I would insist that we put this oral defense off to another time. Believe me, Crystal. This exam is a mere formality. We are all impressed with your diligence and effort."

"What about Dr. Freeman? Is she impressed?"

"She's a pain in the posterior," he confided under his breath. "But you can handle her objections. She's not as expert as you in the field of language dysfluency."

Crystal tried a smile, but her lips felt numb. It seemed a tremendous effort just to stay alert. "Thank you for your concern, Dr. MacConnell."

He patted her back and joined his colleagues in the examination room.

Crystal checked her wristwatch, the lovely timepiece Luke had given her. There were still a few minutes until the hour. Perhaps a splash of cold water would resuscitate her. She headed for the ladies room down the hall, leaving instructions with the secretary that she would be right back.

Standing over the sink, Crystal doused a paper towel in cool water. As she applied it to her forehead, the memory of a mountain stream washed through her. There were chill caverns, waterfalls and a precipitous tumble. She closed her weary eyes and saw the ceiling fan above her bed, lazily rotating while Luke lay beside her. "Now is not the time to act like a love-sick calf," she told the limp reflection in the mirror. "Concentrate."

A rap on the door startled her. A dear, familiar voice asked, "Crystal? Are you all right?"

Luke! Was it actually him or another fantasy. She dared not trust her ears.

"What are you doing? Hanging wallpaper?" the voice persisted.

She flew through the door and into his arms, almost bowling him over with the enthusiasm of her embrace. Not trusting herself to speak, she held up her left hand and showed him the glittering diamond ring.

"My dearest Amber Lady," he breathed softly, "how I love you."

His eyes spoke a secret communication known only to lovers and filled her with strong, abiding confidence. Luke believed in her. Crystal was sure of that. And he cared. Why else would he appear unsummoned at the moment when she most needed his support?

"This is possibly the most important moment of my life," she said. Her amber eyes sparkled with renewed energy. Every nerve tingled. Her spirit revived at the sight and the touch of him. "And all I could think about was you."

"Sounds to me like you've finally got your priorities straight," he teased.

Behind them, the department secretary politely cleared her throat. "Ms Baxter? The committee is waiting."

"Thank you." Crystal smoothed her skirt and adjusted her blazer.

"You look lovely," Luke said.

Crystal's mouth pulled into a mock frown. "That wasn't the effect I was after."

"Then allow me to amend my compliment." He held her face in both hands and punctuated each praise with a pat on both cheeks. "You look beautifully efficient. Gorgeously professional. And charmingly intelligent."

He balled his hand into a fist and gently tapped the point of her out-thrust chin. "Give 'em hell, lady."

She went on tiptoe to plant a quick kiss on his lips. Her expression was joyful and touched with awe. "You've saved my life, Luke. I don't know what Fate brought you here to me, but I bless the force that did. I don't ever want to go through another day without you."

The secretary summoned her again. "Ms Baxter? They are ready for you now."

Crystal gazed into Luke's eyes. "Wait for me?"

"Now and always."

Head high, the true Crystal Baxter sallied forth to meet her inquisitors. Gone was the sad, stumbling reflection of this competent, intelligent woman. Her upright posture radiated confidence. Her hand did not shake. As the door to the conference room closed behind her, she managed one final wink in Luke's direction.

He winked back, taking a lover's pride in her beauty, wit and accomplishment. He silently thanked that provident Fate—in the person of Ginger MacKay—who had caused him to arrive like the cavalry in the nick of time.

He had not needed to be reminded of the moment for Crystal's oral defense. That hour was indelibly printed in his mind. He had fidgeted at his desk, watching the minutes drag slowly by. The thought of lunch flickered to life and was rejected. How could he eat when he knew Crystal was so miserable. He was far less concerned with his own imminent ordeal with the press than with her final examination.

He was vaguely aware of a disturbance in his outer office and assumed that the television crews had arrived early. He had intended to speak from behind his wide oak desk with the backdrop of a vast legal library to underscore his sincerity. It had been a tedious week as he endured the cynicism of critics and the disappointment of his friends, but all he could think about was Crystal.

The door to his office was flung open, and Ginger sailed through like a determined little tugboat. "I'm going to speak to Luke," she shouted to a distraught Ms Baumann. "And you're not going to stop me."

"I'm calling the security guard," Ms Baumann threatened. "Who do you think you are? Shoving in here without an appointment?"

Forcing the amusement from his eyes, Luke crossed

the plush, chocolate-brown carpet. "It's all right, Ms Baumann." He held out his hand. "How are you, Ginger?"

"More p-p-perceptive than you are." She pumped his hand. "Now get rid of this dragon. She wouldn't let me talk with you on the phone, and time is running short."

He waved his protesting secretary from the office. "What's the matter? Is it Crystal?"

"You look as bad as she does. Don't you two ever eat?" She waited for the office door to close. "She stuttered, Luke. I called to wish her luck, and she stuttered."

"There's not a damn thing I can do about it." He held a clenched fist to his lips. "It's all this damn dissertation."

"She needs you, Luke."

The words jumped out at him. She needed him? That was backward. He was always the needy person in their relationship. It gratified him to think he could help her but frightened him, too. What if he failed her? "I don't believe it. Crystal's problem is preexam jitters. She told me last night that she was fine."

Patience was not Ginger's best quality. "People who are fine don't forget to eat and sleep. I didn't drive all the way downtown and pay for a parking space to chat. Get your coat, Luke."

"Wait a minute. She told me that she did *not* need me."

"And I'm telling you different," Ginger said. "She's n-never stuttered before when talking to me. Where's your coat?"

He pointed to the closet in the corner. "What can I do?"

"You can't break life into neat, little compartments. Sure, she's nervous about this exam, but she's also nuts about your relationship. Crystal loves you, and right now she needs your support."

How simple it sounded! Luke knew intuitively that Ginger was right. He grabbed his coat. "Let's go."

He rushed past Ms Baumann. "I'm out for the day."

"What about your press conference?" She waved the neatly typed text of his prepared speech. "Mr. Todhunter, I can't help but comment on this irresponsible behavior."

"Make copies and pass it around," he shouted over his shoulder. "I'm going to do the most responsible thing I've ever done—care for another person."

He raced to the university. The minutes that had dragged now flew in mocking haste. Yet he found her in time.

When he heard her down-hearted voice echoing from the bathroom and saw her first stagger through the door, he knew Ginger had been right. Crystal *was* a woman in need. Her transformation in his arms had convinced him that no matter what other pressures existed, her greatest need was for his love.

As he waited for her he noticed the strained aura among students who drifted in and out of the offices. Almost all of them stopped for a quiet consultation with the departmental secretary, then cast furtive glances at the closed door to the conference room. He realized that Crystal's extreme tension was not such an unusual phenomenon. These students were terrifically keyed up, and they weren't even being tested.

The door to the conference room opened, and Crystal emerged. She was visibly shaken but still confident and more radiant than he had ever seen her—with the possible exception of their lovemaking's aftermath.

Ignoring her fellow students, she went straight to her lover and said with a relaxed grin, "It's over. I've done all I can, and now we just wait for the final verdict."

She sat beside him quietly and grasped his hand. "What do you say to a ten-inch pizza when I'm done."

"Great. But that's a cheap celebration."

"That depends on where and how the pizza is eaten," she leered. "Besides, celebrations might not be in order. Maybe I should put in an order for hemlock, in case I don't pass."

He squeezed her hand.

"Hey, Todhunter. I thought you had a press conference."

"I left it in the capable hands of Ms Baumann. She's a better politician than I am, anyway."

Crystal wrinkled her nose. Gradually, her wan face was returning to its natural color. "I wouldn't give her two points on a charisma scale."

"But she's dedicated. She really cares what the media says."

"And you don't?"

"There's only one person's opinion that matters to me."

The oak door to the conference room opened and Crystal stood to meet Dr. MacConnell. His expression betrayed no emotion. He regarded her solemnly, then slowly extended his hand. "Congratulations, Dr. Baxter."

Despite a sudden weakening of the knees, Crystal kept her voice level. "Thank you, sir."

"Call me Jack," he offered with a smile. "Your defense was quite impressive, and we are now equals."

From a rear office, a whoop of joy resounded. A tape recorder blared the graduation march from *Pomp and Circumstance*, and a mob of graduate students surrounded Crystal. She kept a tight grip on Luke while accepting their excited congratulations.

Though not exactly hoisted on their shoulders, Crystal's sense of triumph was the same. She had been in their position and knew that the award of a doctoral degree was ample cause for celebration. One of their number had emerged victorious. Her success gave hope to them all.

The invitation passed from mouth to mouth. "Party at the Student Union!"

Swept along with the crowd, Crystal glanced over her shoulder at Luke, making sure he was a part of the group. He waved and nodded and calmly followed along. Though this was her milieu, he made himself comfortable and was immediately accepted— much more quickly than she had been while riding the bandwagon of his campaign. *All that charm really deserves a political forum*, she thought, but she was grateful for circumstances that had caused him to withdraw.

The celebration at the Student Union was raucous, and Crystal cheerfully accepted the unstinting support shown to her by her colleagues. Their outpouring of friendly good wishes was gratifying, but all the while, she was anticipating the private celebration with Luke that was yet to come.

She offered one final toast and departed with him, noting that the students' farewells had included Luke.

Her face was now flushed with excitement. Outside, in the red-streaked sunset, she turned to him. "Would you drive? I don't trust myself."

"You only had two beers. I was counting."

"I'm drunk with relief, not alcohol." She tucked her arm into his and they strolled across the campus in companionable silence.

Finally, she said, "I'm almost sorry it's over. I'm going to miss this place."

"You could start over," he suggested. "Aim for an advanced degree in anthropology or physics or botany."

"I said *almost*," Crystal protested, waving her hands to ward off the work load he so willingly thrust upon her. "I'm not a professional student."

When they found his car—ticketed with a summons from the campus police—she offered a hint of the specialty she would like to learn more about. "What I really need is an advanced field study in anatomy."

"What qualifications are you seeking in a teacher?" he asked, opening the passenger door and stowing the parking ticket in his glove compartment.

She waited for his complete attention. "Blue eyes are a must. Blond hair." She reached to tweak the rebellious lock that fell across his forehead. Her hands slid to his shoulders. "I'd want my teacher to be broad here." She measured and drew her hands away describing the width of his shoulder span. "But narrow here." She touched his torso. "Slim hips, firm behind, long legs, lots of muscles."

She backed away and announced, "I think you'd do rather well. Are you available?"

He trapped her in the circle of his arms and joined her against him at the hip. "I might be. But you

should know that I am offering this course with one
very important requirement."

"A prerequisite?"

"Absolutely." His expression turned serious. There
was still a lilting note to his voice, but Crystal deduced the deeper meaning of his words. She knew her
answer was very important.

"You might say that I'm insisting on a completion
of the course. I want to add an M-r-s. to your Ph.D.
Are you willing?"

Crystal had a reply on the tip of her tongue—"not
yet." That was the reflex response she'd given for so
many years. Her life-style had revolved around the fulfillment of her degree, and she was about to react almost automatically. A parade of past refusals marched
before her—a big brass band that replayed an endless
refrain of "never, never, never."

Now it was over. The music faded, and she joyously
waved farewell to the brass drum that pounded a
"no" with every beat. Her mind was as still as a
mountain glen. In her frenzied quest for academic
recognition, she had always denied herself the quiet
pleasure of the first robin's wakening song. What a
wonderful future could be hers!

"My father used to say . . . ."

He groaned, but she continued. "My father used to
say, like L.B. Mayer, that a verbal contract is not
worth the paper it's written on. But I don't believe
that. I fully intend to live up to my answer."

He squeezed her tiny waist and said sarcastically,
"You're so romantic."

"Well, this isn't exactly roses and candlelight, Luke
You're proposing—you are proposing, aren't you?—
in a parking lot."

He dropped to one knee, eliciting sidelong glances from the student pedestrians on their way to the library or the union or evening studies. "Will you marry me, Amber Lady? Will you share your life with me?"

"Will I bear your children and bake your bread?"

"Do we have to get specific?"

"I guess we could formalize later," she said. "In any case, the answer is...yes."

"Is that a 'yes'?" he asked with a widening grin. "Yes? You will join your name with mine?"

"With a hyphen," she said. A glow of satisfaction colored her face as she gazed down into his idiotic grin. Could it be possible that this man who had been courted by senators in Washington and by the local press was the same lighthearted lunatic that knelt before her? "What would your law partners say if they could see you now?"

"There's only one proper response—congratulations!" He bounded to his feet and grabbed a passing student. "Excuse me, young man, but I need a witness. This lady has just agreed to marry me."

The student pushed his hair out of his eyes for a better look at Crystal. His appreciation was evident in his prolonged gaze. "Congratulations, man."

"Thank you." Luke shook his hand and sent him on his way. "You see? That's the only right thing to say."

She took his hands in hers before his enthusiasm could again overflow onto innocent bystanders. "Now, about that anatomy course you recommended? When can we start?"

"I love you even though you are a dirty old lady." With no further ceremony or announcement, he ushered her into the Ferrari and dashed around to his side. Fortunately, a benign justice guided his route, and Luke received no traffic citations for speeding. In record time, he found a parking place in the street in front of Crystal's Victorian home.

He rushed her up to the threshold, impatiently tapping his foot while she fumbled for her keys. The dash up the wide, carved stairs leading to her bedroom was accomplished with equal haste. Clothing was torn from their impatient bodies, and finally—with a long, satisfied sigh—Luke flopped beside her on the four-poster bed. They lay on their naked backs, inches apart, and stared at the ceiling fan.

Though they had shared her bed before, a touching nervousness filled them. They were engaged, and it made a difference. Crystal cleared her throat. "Mr. Todhunter? If you intend to hurry through the rest of this course like you raced here, I might consider changing professors."

He laughed. "I wanted to get you into the classroom before you had a change of heart."

"Not likely." She watched the rise and fall of his chest. "Of course, we'll live here. At my house."

"Isn't this your parents' house?"

"Yes, but they'll be gone for at least another year." She trailed her foot up his leg. "Besides, my office is so convenient here."

"Too much so," he replied pensively. "I can't take the chance you'll meet another stutterer like me."

"You're not going to be the jealous type, are you?"

"You bet." His hand strayed absently to her thigh. "I want you to be mine. All mine. We'll shop for our own house."

"Not a condo," she insisted, "but a house. A real house with a front door and a porch and a basement."

"Is this a course in real estate?" he growled. "Or a lesson in love."

He leaned above her, gazing into her tawny eyes. His breath felt warm on her cheek as he gently lowered himself, meeting her soft, female body with his male hardness. "Does it matter where we live?"

"Not really. As long as it's exactly what I want." Her arms encircled his neck. "You know, Luke. I don't feel any different."

"Different from what?"

"Well, I expected that when I got that handshake, I'd change. And when I accepted your proposal, I figured there would be some dramatic transformation." She grinned. "Like my freckles would disappear or my hair would suddenly fall into smooth, straight waves."

"I'm glad you didn't change, Amber Lady. I love you the way you are. Especially the freckles." He kissed the spots on her nose. "Only the years will change us. Will you still love me when I'm fat and fifty?"

"Will you still love me when I'm a pompous, old fool?"

The answers were given in the joining of thigh to thigh. Their speechless lips told the eternal story of a man and a woman and a loving embrace. Each caress made a vow, and their kisses sealed the promise of their freedom together.

EPILOGUE

CRYSTAL'S KNEES WERE QUIVERY. Her lips were dry, and her eyes refused to focus. Loud organ music resounded through the oak-paneled anteroom.

Her sisters, Garnet and Jade, were dressed in floor-length bridesmaids' frocks of forest-green velvet for the January wedding. They chattered and hugged Crystal encouragingly, but it was Ginger—also in forest green—who straightened her filmy veil. "You look so beautiful, Dr. Baxter."

"Umph," Crystal replied.

"Don't talk, honey. Just look at yourself in the mirror."

Crystal barely recognized the vision. Her great-grandmother's ivory satin dress with antique lace fit her tiny waist perfectly. The mandarin collar emphasized her graceful neck. Long, leg-of-mutton sleeves ended in points at her wrists. It was a turn-of-the-century design that fell in a straight panel of lace at the front and gathered at the back for a bustle, one tradition Crystal had decided to forego.

Her mother appeared in the mirror, reflected with a soft smile and glowing amber-flecked eyes. "I'm so glad you chose January to get married," she said. "I'd much rather be here than in an Alaskan igloo."

Ginger commented, "I don't know how you stand the cold, Mrs. Baxter."

"My hearth is always pleasant," she said warmly, still regarding her daughter in the mirror. "A good book, cup of cocoa and loving husband almost make the long winters fun."

"Mom!" Jade shouted disapprovingly.

"Well, I couldn't remember if I'd ever told Crystal about the birds and bees. I just wanted her to know it was...fun."

Jade wrapped her arms around her mother and squeezed. "She would have been more definitive, Crystal. But she's been hanging around dad too long."

The organist—Mr. Pappas who adored repetitive refrains—paused dramatically, then began the traditional wedding march.

Ginger led Crystal to the door where her father waited. The tall, thin gentleman looked dignified in his black frock coat and striped trousers. An overhead light reflected on his shiny, bald pate. He took his daughter's hand and folded it protectively over his arm.

"The rocks at the bottom of a stream always look brilliant," he whispered, "but only pure gold keeps its sparkle in the sun."

Crystal nodded wisely, and they joined the wedding procession.

Everyone was there—from a beaming Marv at the deli to a staid, proper Ms Baumann. As Crystal passed each fragrantly garlanded aisle, she caught a glimpse of her life. Dr. MacConnell winked. Jason and Everett, her two impish students from the Children's Museum, were fidgeting uncomfortably in their neat little suits. When she passed, they grinned and gave her the thumbs-up sign. Childhood friends, therapy clients, campaign workers and student colleagues all beamed as Crystal and her father marched slowly by.

At the end of the aisle on the groom's side, Luke's mother reigned. A dominating power was evident in her athletically erect posture and the proud set of her head. Pure-white hair was arranged Oriental style. Her ice-blue eyes riveted on Crystal, and slowly her lips curved in an approving smile. With a slight nod, she officially recognized her new daughter-in-law.

Luke stepped forward to claim his bride. When their hands met, Crystal trembled. He was dashing in a dark frock coat tailored to accommodate his broad shoulders. With his pearl-gray cravat and diamond stickpin, he could have stepped from another era—a more romantic time—to greet his Amber Lady.

In his eyes she saw the clear blue horizon of a loving future. Together, they took their place before the rotund, red-faced minister.

"Dearly beloved..." he intoned, his Texas accent far less obvious in person than on the tapes Crystal listened to so frequently.

When he came to the exchange of vows, his forehead wrinkled in anxious concern. "Repeat after me: I, Crystal Jane Baxter...."

"I-I-I-I C-c-c-crystale...."

With a nod, he turned to Luke. "You may kiss the bride."

It only took a feather-light touch of his lips to release her, and she firmly repeated, "I, Crystal Jane Baxter take Luke William Todhunter...."

BARBARA DELINSKY

Fingerprints

Carly Quinn is a
woman with a past.
Born Robyn Hart, she
was forced to don a new
identity when her intensive
investigation of an arson-ring
resulted in a photographer's death
and threats against her life.

Ryan Cornell's entrance into her life
was a gradual one. The handsome
lawyer's interest was piqued, and then
captivated, by the mysterious Carly—a
woman of soaring passions and a
secret past.

Introducing

Harlequin Temptation ™

Sensuous…contemporary…compelling…reflecting today's love relationships! The passionate torment of a woman torn between two loves…the siren call of a career… the magnetic advances of an impetuous employer–nothing is left unexplored in this romantic new series from Harlequin. You'll thrill to a candid new frankness as men and women seek to form lasting relationships in the face of temptations that threaten true love. *Don't miss a single one!* You can start new *Harlequin Temptation* coming to *your* home each month for just $1.75 per book–a saving of 20¢ off the suggested retail price of $1.95. Begin with your FREE copy of *First Impressions.* Mail the reply card today!

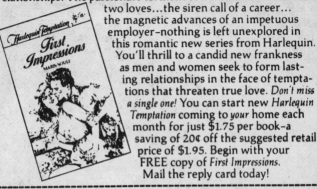

1. How do you rate _____ ?
   (Please print book TITLE)
   1.6 ☐ excellent   .4 ☐ good   .2 ☐ not so good
   .5 ☐ very good   .3 ☐ fair   .1 ☐ poor

2. How likely are you to purchase another book in this series?
   2.1 ☐ definitely would purchase   .3 ☐ probably would not purchase
   .2 ☐ probably would purchase   .4 ☐ definitely would not purchase

3. How do you compare this book with similar books you usually read?
   3.1 ☐ far better than others   .4 ☐ not as good
   .2 ☐ better than others   .5 ☐ definitely not as good
   .3 ☐ about the same

   V12

4. Have you any additional comments about this book?
   _____ (4)
   _____ (6)

5. How did you *first* become aware of this book?
   8. ☐ read other books in series   11. ☐ friend's recommendation
   9. ☐ in-store display   12. ☐ ad inside other books
   10. ☐ TV, radio or magazine ad   13. ☐ other _____
      (please specify)

6. What *most* prompted you to buy this book?
   14. ☐ read other books in series   17. ☐ title   20. ☐ story outline on back
   15. ☐ friend's recommendation   18. ☐ author   21. ☐ read a few pages
   16. ☐ picture on cover   19. ☐ advertising   22. ☐ other _____
      (please specify)

7. What type(s) of paperback fiction have you purchased in the past 3 months? Approximately how many?

	No. purchased		No. purchased
☐ contemporary romance	(23) ___	☐ espionage	(37) ___
☐ historical romance	(25) ___	☐ western	(39) ___
☐ gothic romance	(27) ___	☐ contemporary novels	(41) ___
☐ romantic suspense	(29) ___	☐ historical novels	(43) ___
☐ mystery	(31) ___	☐ science fiction/fantasy	(45) ___
☐ private eye	(33) ___	☐ occult	(47) ___
☐ action/adventure	(35) ___	☐ other	(49) ___

8. Have you purchased any books from any of these Harlequin Series in the past 3 months? Approximately how many?

	No. Purchased		No. Purchased
☐ Romance	(51) ___	☐ Superromance	(57) ___
☐ Presents	(53) ___	☐ Temptation	(59) ___
☐ American Romance	(55) ___		

9. On which date was this book purchased? (61) _____

10. Please indicate your age group and sex.
    63.1 ☐ Male   64.1 ☐ under 15   .3 ☐ 25-34   .5 ☐ 50-64
    .2 ☐ Female   .2 ☐ 15-24   .4 ☐ 35-49   .6 ☐ 65 or older

Thank you for completing and returning this questionnaire.

NAME _____
ADDRESS _____
(Please Print)
CITY _____
ZIP CODE _____

BUSINESS REPLY MAIL
FIRST CLASS   PERMIT NO. 70   TEMPE, AZ.

POSTAGE WILL BE PAID BY ADDRESSEE

NATIONAL READER SURVEYS

2504 West Southern Avenue
Tempe, AZ   85282